Christmas in Bonaire

Also by Anne Bennett

I invite you to read my trilogy,

A Lyle Cooper Story. Just a splash of spice in this three book series.

On Bonaire

Back to Bonaire

My Bonaire

The Diner on Bonaire

Coming 2025

Christmas in Bonaire

A Bonaire Island Novel

Anne Bennett

Cover Design: GetCovers

Author photo: Amanda Cramp

Copyright © 2024 by Anne Bennett

ISNB eBook 979-8-9864896-8-1

ISBN paperback 979-8-9864896-9-8

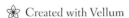 Created with Vellum

For my mom, Joan Bennett Dobricki. She was the magic of Christmas.

Chapter One

"This damned snow." Annie Martis sat on her butt in the middle of the icy pathway in Central Park. "Argh." The sun was just coming up over the skyscrapers that encircled the square. Thankfully, at this early hour, there was no one around to witness her second slip and fall of the morning. Her cell buzzed in her pocket and she checked the caller ID. She touched Decline. "Sorry Greet," she mumbled, "bad timing."

She struggled to her feet, pulled her cap down over her ears, and took off at a cautious jog. She was determined to complete her daily run no matter the weather. The snow crunched below her feet as she intentionally placed each step. As she made her way, the icy air bit her nose and burned her lungs. Her eyes were watering and her lips had turned dry when she made the turn for home. With her targeted three miles behind her, she fell to a walk and hurried up the street. She checked the time and saw she was running ten minutes late. "This damned snow."

"Isn't it beautiful out here?" a chirpy passerby said. "There's nothing like a fresh snowfall to lift your spirits."

"Right." Annie tried to grin but her cheeks were stiff from the cold and she only managed a grimace. She begrudgingly looked around, willing to study her surroundings from the stranger's point of view. The trees were covered in white and the sky a clear blue. The snow brought a certain crispness to the air and a feeling of being elsewhere. The familiar neighborhood now a new landscape. The sun bounced off the towering buildings and the ground sparkled. "Beautiful?" She considered the word. "I don't think so. A huge inconvenience, yes. I'll be glad for spring and green grass underfoot."

Arriving at the brownstone, she took the eight steps two at a time. Her Aunt Peggy had hung a Neiman Marcus Christmas spray on each of the double doors. The nontraditional pink and gold stood out against the rich mahogany panels sure to draw attention from anyone passing by.

Once inside, she kicked off her running shoes and dashed down the stairs to her basement apartment. An heirloom knit stocking hung from the mantel, the only sign in the place that Christmas was nearing. She hadn't hung the sock but had an idea who did. Walking passed the coffee maker she pushed Brew and went to start the shower.

After a quick wash, she sipped her coffee and stood in front of the mirror. She brushed and dried her long brunette hair until it laid flat against her head. Pulling it all into a tight bun, she secured it at the back of her neck. Checking her reflection, she turned left, then right ensuring every lock was in place. A bit of mascara and not too much blush, she added a pale rose lip color then checked her teeth for smudges.

The closet in her bedroom was filled with blue and black suits. The hangers sat two inches apart. She stood in front of the line of clothing and studied her choices. Would it be a pant or a skirt today? Not a hard decision since she simply alternated between the two. Once dressed, she placed her empty mug in the dishwasher, slipped her feet into her heels and went back up the stairs.

"There she is," her Uncle Joe said. "Good morning, Annie. Have a seat. Eggs are ready." He slid two over-easy onto a plate. She couldn't help but notice, since his retirement, her uncle had turned into an easy going guy, and a bit of a couch potato. But he couldn't break the habit of getting up before dawn.

"I'm running late," Annie said. "Don't bother with the toast." She sat and salted her eggs. Her aunt, seated next to her, was finishing her breakfast. "Thanks for hanging the stocking, Aunt Peggy."

"I thought your little place needed some holiday cheer," she said. "When you have a minute, we need to talk about Christmas."

"What do you want to discuss?" Annie snapped her linen napkin open and placed it on her lap.

"I can't decide between The Waverly Inn and Rolfs. Both have spectacular Christmas Eve menus. The Waverly is doing the beef tartare with capers, but Rolfs has the most delicious Duck bon bons. If I don't get a reservation made today, we may be scurrying for bits like field mice."

"They both sound great, I don't think you can go wrong. You and Uncle Joe should decide." She checked the time. "Dang, I'm late." She added pepper then cut into her eggs.

"Okay then, I think I'll call Rolfs, they have such beautiful decorations. Will it be just the three of us or should I get a table for four?"

"Make it four. Stewart's parents are in Europe." She glanced at the ring on her finger. "I invited him to join us for the holiday and he was delighted."

"How are things at the office?" Uncle Joe asked. He placed his plate on the table and sat. "Getting any nearer to closing that enormous deal?"

"We're this close. We have a final meeting this morning." She took another bite. "If this merger goes through, I may be able to move out of your basement. Stewart and I could start looking for a place of our own. You'll finally be rid of me."

"Nonsense," Uncle Joe said. "Merger or not, you'll always have a home here. And that offer for you and your future husband to stay in the apartment downstairs still stands."

"You're both too good to me." She stood, rinsed her plate, and checked the time. "Thanks for the eggs." She kissed her uncle on his cheek. "I'm running late. Fingers crossed this snow isn't affecting the subway schedule."

———

Just as Annie had suspected, due to the weather the line was running late. Wrapped in a designer wool coat and with a scarf covering her nose, after a forty minute commute, she emerged from the underground onto Wall Street. She checked the time and picked up her step. Her feet flew over the recently cleared sidewalk, the ice and snow pushed to the street. The energy of the city pulsed around her like a familiar friend. She swiped at the snowflakes that landed on her eyelashes and adjusted her leather gloves.

Business people carrying briefcases and wearing laptop-laden backpacks rushed over the crowded sidewalks. All most likely running as late as Annie due to the wintery weather.

"Excuse me, pardon," she called out, overtaking several with her long stride. As she approached a monstrous glass door with *Global World Bank* etched in gold leaf, a gentleman pulled it open for her. He'd been working at the bank long before Annie joined on and helped people through the door from opening to close. For the past four years, she could count on a smile and a nod from the man as she arrived at the bank. In spite of wearing a heavy winter coat and cap, his nose had grown red and he sniffled. "Thank you..." she tried to remember the doorman's name but it escaped her, "so much."

The financial institute's main office took up an entire New York block. Her heels clicked over the marble floor as she sped to catch the lift. She nodded at strangers who filled the elevator, claimed the spot at the front, then stared at the numbers overhead. *Santa Baby* jingled from the hidden speakers. The happy tune seemed somehow off, drifting over the stiff collared financiers. Her cell buzzed. She checked the caller ID and touched Decline for the second time that morning. Her best friend would have to wait. As they rose, she patted her head making sure her hair was smooth and no pieces had escaped her bun.

After two verses, the doors swooshed open on the seventeenth floor. Her assistant stood just outside. Annie gave the woman her coat and scarf as they walked toward her office.

"They're waiting for you," her assistant said.

"Thank you, Virginia." Annie pivoted and headed toward the boardroom.

"You can call me Ginny." She said, as she watched her boss walk away.

"Miss Martis, wonderful." Richard, her supervisor, greeted her as she entered the room. He seemed relieved that she had arrived. He addressed the business professionals murmuring among themselves. "We can get started now."

The conference room table sat sixteen and was full when Annie took her seat at the head. "I apologize for being late." She addressed the anxious group while opening her laptop. "This awful snow is really hampering my schedule."

———

"Annie, great work today." Richard gave two raps on her office door as he walked in. His smile was genuine and she found his look of relief comical. She was always thankful for his positive feedback. Annie had been working under Richard for years and with each of her successes, he gave her more profitable clients. As a team they had become invaluable to the mergers and acquisitions department.

"I think so too," she said. "Once they crunch the numbers we gave them, they're bound to see how lucrative this union will be. Add the minimal risk involved and I'm confident we'll have them signing on the bottom line soon after the holidays."

"And when that happens," Richard said, "you'll be promoted to Associate, congratulations. You've really earned it, Annie, I'm proud of you. I don't have to tell you it comes with a hefty salary increase and the corner office."

"I'm ready. I've had my eye on this promotion since day one. I've proven myself more than capable. When this client signs and the deal is finalized, I'll get my due reward." Her cell rang and she checked the caller ID.

"Go ahead and take that. I just wanted to stop in and congratulate you."

"It's not important." She touched Decline. "Tell the procurement team I'll have these new figures over to them by the end of the day."

"Don't you have Christmas shopping to do or a tree to decorate? You've been working around the clock getting today's presentation ready. Take a break. Go hug your fiancé. He may not even recognize you."

"Thanks Richard, but I'll feel a whole lot better when I know we've got this merger in the can. I just want to make sure I haven't left any loose threads. When we come back after the new year, I want to slide into home plate and be done with this."

"Okay then, I'll leave you to it. I'm off to the Hamptons for the holiday. I'll see you in January. Have a merry Christmas."

But she didn't hear him. She was already deep in the spreadsheet.

A knock on her office door pulled Annie out of her zone. She was surprised to see the sun had set.

"Come in Virginia." She straightened and pulled her shoulders back. "What can I do for you?"

"I just wanted to say goodnight." She placed a pretty package on Annie's desk. "And give you this."

"For me?" Annie opened the envelope and removed a card. An animated elf held a sign over its head with *Merry Christmas Boss* written on it. She opened it and read the message. "Virginia, this is so nice."

"I go by Ginny."

"Thank you." She delicately removed the green wrapping paper from the box and examined the gift. It was a game called, *Never Have I Ever.*

"I hope you like it. My tribe and I had a blast playing it. We were up until all hours during our girls' night. I thought maybe you'd like to give it a go with your friends."

"I'm afraid I don't have a reciprocal to offer. I thought the bonus—"

"Oh, sure. No, I don't mean to—" She smiled. "Merry Christmas Miss Martis. I'll see you after the first of the year."

Annie saved then closed the documents she had been working on and shut her computer. She looked at the gift and wondered if Aunt Peggy and Uncle Joe would like to play. Maybe Stewart would join in. Her phone vibrated. This time she touched Accept.

"Greet, what a nice surprise. How are things on Bonaire?" She waited but got no reply. "Hello? Greet, are you there?" She heard sniffling followed by an uncomfortable snicker. "Greet you're making me nervous. Say something."

"He left me."

Chapter Two

S tewart twirled angel hair around his fork. Annie admired the way the candlelight flickered off his sharp profile. One lone strand of hair fell over his forehead. He had just left his office and was still in his suit and tie. She studied the French onion soup in the crock in front of her, waiting for it to cool.

"I don't understand how you can call her your best friend," he said. "You haven't seen her in years."

"We've known each other since the day we were born. Our mothers were besties and raised us practically as sisters. Ten years is a lot of time, but it can't break the bonds of sisterhood."

"All I'm saying is, it's hard to keep up a friendship when you're so far away. I never see my old college buddies any more. I consider them past friends."

"My mom went into labor with me the same day Greet's parents brought her home from the hospital. They used to push us side by side in our strollers. There's a picture somewhere of the two of us getting our first haircut together." She remembered the small home she grew up in and wondered whatever happened to that photo.

"We're still best friends." It had to be true, otherwise, who would currently qualify as a friend? She'd always been such a workhorse, it left little time for relationship building. Without Greet, Annie knew she fell into the completely friendless category.

"Okay, if you say so," he said. "She never left the island?"

"No, she still lives on Bonaire in the town we grew up in. It sounds like she's having marital problems and is looking for support. She's invited me to come and stay with her and her daughter. I can't decide if I should go or not." She lifted a spoonful of cheesy croutons in broth and watched the steam rise from it. "I don't understand what's going on down there. Greet and Puck have been together since we were teens."

"When exactly was the last time you saw her?"

"It was the day of my mother's funeral." She rested the spoon on the side of the bowl. "After the ceremony, Aunt Peggy and Uncle Joe wasted no time in bringing me here. He had his job to get back to. Saying goodbye to Greet, I felt like I was leaving half of me behind."

Annie remembered that day. It was so much more than just leaving her best friend. Bonaire was her home. She hardly had time to see all the people who had been part of her early life. School chums, her mother's friends, and her boyfriend all received a fleeting glimpse and a wave before she packed a few bags and boarded a plane to the states.

"That must've been tough on you," Stewart said. "Having to start all over at seventeen. In New York City of all places." His phone buzzed. "Excuse me, I should take this." He touched his screen and smiled across the table at his fiancé. He spoke to the caller, "Stewart here." He listened. "No, not at all. What can I do for you?" He rolled his eyes and Annie giggled. "I'm not available to volunteer at this time, but I'd be glad to make a financial contribution." Winking at her, he wrapped up the call. "I'm happy to help. I'll have my assistant call you. Merry Christmas to you as well." He slid the cell into his jacket's inner pocket. "That's why you want to have money," he said.

"I just bought myself out of having to serve dinners at the shelter over on 3rd Street." He picked up his fork. "I'm sorry, Annie. What were you saying?"

"We were talking about when I first came to New York." She tasted her soup.

"Yes, go on, please." He began twirling another forkful.

"I traded one island for another. I didn't appreciate it at the time, but I've had so many opportunities here. I guess if I were still on that tiny island in the Caribbean, I'd be—" She smiled, "I can't even picture it. I certainly wouldn't be looking at Associate and working on Wall Street."

"Maybe you'd be selling bananas to tourists out of the back of your banger. Car parked on the side of an unpaved road wearing a tie-dyed shirt and cut-offs. Can you imagine?"

The comment rubbed her wrong but she plastered a smile on her face. What did Stewart know about the people on Bonaire? She let it slide, after all, he may be right. She remembered tooting around town in her father's beat up truck. Saltwater and the island sun combined to rust a hole right through the floorboard. Talk about a banger.

Her father used to yell, "high water ahead," and she'd lift her feet as they drove over a puddle. The bed was often filled with coolers of ice and recently caught fish. Annie learned early on how to cut and fillet them. At first, she was hesitant. The sad dark eyes looked up at her and she only wished she could set them free again.

One day, her father sat her down and explained the circle of life. He then told her even Jesus caught fish to feed his flock. He said, "If it's okay for the good Lord, do you think eating fish is okay for us too?" Her dad waited patiently as she worked it out. Finally, she nodded and he patted her back. "Now toss those guts to the seagulls. They have babies to feed." With a grin on her face, the sky lit up with squawking birds and bloody innards. Each day she'd join him on his delivery route and they would plan for the next day's catch. Where did they think the fish would be biting?

"Do whatever you think is best," Stewart said. "If you want to make the trip, that's fine with me." He squinted and cocked his head. "Did you want me to go with you?"

"You ask that like it would be a terrible thing."

"That's not what I meant. It's pretty remote there and I may need to keep in touch with the campaign. Do you think they have Wi-Fi?"

"I'm sure they do," she hedged. "I don't know how reliable it is. Anyway, it's so close to Christmas. Traveling to the island could be a real bear. I'll tell Greet I can't come. I'm sure she'll understand." She dipped her spoon and took another taste of the soup. "I'm so busy at the bank. It would be hard for me to get away."

"I thought you were wrapping up that project. Then it's Associate with the sweet new office. You've worked so hard for this. It's finally all coming together."

"It looks like they're going to sign after the first of the year." She dabbed the corner of her mouth. "It's a fantastic merger for our client and will pay off big time for me. This is really a bad time to be taking a trip to Bonaire." There were so many reasons not to go but something wouldn't leave her. An annoying pull kept her second guessing her decision. Picturing herself on a sandy beach with sunlight beaming down, she could feel her shoulders relax just imagining it.

"If you don't want to go, I'm sure Greet can find someone who can help her," he said. "She's been fine all these years without you."

"But it's not the same as having a best friend there, not when her marriage is at stake. I've never even met her daughter. Nel's eight already."

"You should go then. I thought your department at the bank was closing down over the holidays."

"The office is closed, Richard's at the Hamptons, but that doesn't mean I don't still have work to do." She watched the flame flicker and the pull to see Greet grew.

"That's my Annie." He refilled her wine glass. "You're a bulldozer. It's just as well you stay home then."

"Maybe you and I can take a day trip out to the island. We can visit the tree farms and see the Christmas lights."

"I don't think I'll have the time," Stewart said. "The campaign I'm working on is set to go into high gear. Our candidate has a very real chance of becoming the next governor of this great state. When she wins, there's a good possibility she'll appoint me lead counsel. Who knows? You may one day be married to a high-ranking politician."

"That's the plan." She grinned. "By that time, I hope to have made vice president. Sure, I'm excited about this next promotion, but I certainly won't settle on it being my last. After a couple years as associate, I'll get the VP position, then senior VP. One day, managing director, just like Uncle Joe."

Annie and Stewart had met their Junior year at New York University. Annie was following in her uncle's footsteps and working toward a double major in accounting and finance. Stewart was a top student in the business and political economy department. They were both scholastically driven and neither enjoyed college antics. Fun and games would only get in the way of top grades. They met while studying in the campus library late one Friday night.

After graduation they planned to stay in New York. Manhattan offered connections not available in other parts of the world. Individuals at the top of their game strolled these streets and Annie and Stewart wanted to work and live among them. With their degrees from the prestigious private university in hand, the level of success they could achieve in the city was immeasurable.

"Is Greet coming to our wedding?" Stewart asked. "I'd love to meet this best friend slash sister."

"No, I'm afraid our guest list is limited," she said. "Just family, business partners, some associates from the bank, your campaign staff and candidates." She took a sip of her wine and fell back in her chair. "I've committed to helping get the invitations in the mail. Seems a little barbaric, sending paper invites through an outdated delivery system, but my aunt insists on it. She thinks e-mail would be too cold."

"There's the woman I love. Fighting tradition every step of the way."

"I can't justify the time hand addressing three hundred envelopes will take."

"You just said our list was limited."

"Yes, limited to—"

"Just say it, Annie. On our wedding day, we'll be surrounded by five or six family members who love us unconditionally and a few hundred people we hardly know but who can—"

"Influence our careers in a positive direction. Yes, I'm aware."

Central Park was a buzz with activity. The new fallen snow called to families who bundled up and headed outside. Parents pulled small children on sleds across the frozen wonderland while Annie watched them from the library in her home. The brownstone was warmed by a blaze dancing in the fireplace. The white lights on the tree were steady. Aunt Peggy never liked the twinkling kind. Annie remembered her making a comment that she thought they looked tacky. The branches were decorated with the likes of Tiffany & Co. and Swarovski's crystals. There was no chance Aunt Peggy could be accused of having tasteless decorations.

Annie stared out the window and remembered helping her mother decorate for Christmas. They would string their tree with colorful sparkling lights and cover it with handmade ornaments. Many of them were made by Annie while still in elementary school. Cotton ball snowmen and toothpick stars. Seashells glued together to form a ring that hung from a ribbon. Each January her mother carefully packed away the priceless decorations and placed the box in the attic. Unlike Aunt Peggy's tree that sat in the corner of the room, their tree on Bonaire was placed on the front porch for everyone in the neighborhood to enjoy. She recalled the feel of her father's massive hand holding hers as they searched through the tree lot for the perfect one. How many trees did he hold while her mother circled around it only to declare it wasn't the right one? Glancing out her New York window, she held her hands to her heart, missing the father she so dearly loved.

The snow-covered families moved out of view and Annie rejoined her aunt at an expansive mahogany desk. A tower of eggshell invitations and matching envelopes were stacked between them. Silver embossed script announced the wedding of Annie Martis to Stewart Woolf. Her uncle stoked the fire and added a log, the room warmed nicely. He sat in his smoking chair and lit a pipe then flipped through his copy of Business Weekly.

"My alumni group got a wind of the wedding," Aunt Peggy said. "So that's six more invitations. It's an ivy league group, so they'll fit in with the other guests just fine." She moved her pen over an envelope. "Annie, you've always had such fine handwriting. I hope my chicken scratch won't embarrass you."

"Don't be silly. I'm grateful to you for helping. I'll get these mailed right after Christmas. It'll be nice to have one less thing to do."

"You still need to decide on your dress. Barbara at the bridal shop said you have to choose between the three you've put on hold. She can't keep them off the sales floor indefinitely. Other brides might want them. You should do it soon. You'll need to leave enough time for alterations."

"I understand. It's just so hard to pick one." She checked the next address on her list and began to write. "I guess I'm having trouble imagining myself walking down the aisle. Would Stewart like me in the mermaid? I think the ball gown may be a bit too much."

"Too much for The Plaza?" She raised her eyebrows. "There's no such thing. The trumpet style dress with the crystal belt is really glamourous. I saw a similar one in the window at Kleinfeld."

"Yes, it's very glamourous. I'd hate to be up staged by my own gown. I'll schedule another appointment with Barbara and definitely decide then."

"I only wish your mother could be here," Uncle Joe said. "She'd be so happy for you and Stewart."

"I was thinking about my mom the other day." Annie slid the card stock into an envelope then drew a line through a name on her list. She wished she could say she often thought of the woman snatched away in the prime of her life. But with the passing of time, memories of her mother found their way into Annie's thoughts less often. It was like trying to hold a snowball in her hand in the hopes of keeping it forever.

"Greet called me. We had a long chat. It happens all the time. After we hang up from our talk, I'm always flooded with memories of my mother and the island. She loved Christmas so much. She had a special way of making the holiday feel magical."

"I'm sure she did," Uncle Joe said. "Everything my sister touched turned into a fairy tale."

"New York is beautiful," Annie said. "But it was different there. On Bonaire, most of the celebrations included the entire town. Huge community dinners and packed church services." She lit up. "I remember one Christmas Eve when I brought Greet a gift. She opened it right before we went inside for the midnight mass. It was one of those groaner tubes we used to play with." She giggled. "I don't know what she was thinking but that thing moaned all through the sermon. Father O'Brian shot her a stink eye that had the entire congregation sitting up straight in the pews."

Annie remembered standing as the choir belted out Away in a Manger. When a long *wwaahh* sounded from behind them, her father's shoulders started to shake. He could hardly contain his laughter. She'd taken his hand and they sang louder, trying to drown out the groaner tube and hide their giggles.

"That sounds just like the two of you," Aunt Peggy said. "I understand you were always up to mischief. How is Greet?"

"Not good. She's having trouble with her marriage. Puck left her."

"What kind of a name is Puck?" Uncle Joe asked.

"No kind." Annie shrugged her shoulders. "Just Puck."

"That's a shame about their marriage," Aunt Peggy said. "Didn't you tell us they have a daughter?"

"Yes, Nel's eight years old." Annie put her pen down and stretched her fingers open and closed. "Greet got pregnant right after high school. Of course, I was living in Manhattan by then. She and Puck had a shotgun wedding. Which sounds unfortunate," she smiled. "But now I'm realizing she never had to hand-address hundreds of invitations."

"I'm so glad the two of you have kept in touch." Uncle Joe closed his magazine then clicked on the television. "The most difficult thing I've ever had to do was move you off that island. You started weeping at your mother's funeral and didn't stop for a month. Peggy and I would hear you upstairs crying yourself to sleep. We were so worried we'd done the wrong thing. It was like dropping a lamb into a pack of wolves the day we brought you to Manhattan."

"You had no choice," Annie said. "It was hard for everyone at the time but look at how it's all turned out. I have morphed from a lamb and am soon to be a Woolf." They smiled. "I can't imagine my life anywhere but here." She resumed writing. "Greets invited me to come and visit. I think she needs a shoulder to cry on."

"You should go," Uncle Joe said. "Now's the perfect time."

"My heart wants to go. But my head keeps reminding me of the legal contracts and all the numbers that need to be rechecked. The office will be nice and quiet over the holidays. I should take advantage of working undisturbed."

"Take some time off and have some fun," he said. "Lord knows you deserve it. When I worked at Global World, I let the business run my life. Gosh, how many weekends did I go into that office? Peggy would call and ask if I was going to make it home before dark. When I had to start taking blood pressure medication, I knew things had to change. Taking early retirement was the best thing for me, I was burnt out. I don't want the same thing to happen to you."

"You don't want me to be successful and financially independent?" Annie teased. "Because that's exactly what happened to you."

"I get your point," he said. "But at what cost? Your Aunt Peggy ate a lot of dinners alone during our marriage. Annie, I'm afraid I inadvertently influenced you into a career in finance. I never would've chosen this life for you. You're twenty-seven, you have a lot of years ahead of you. Don't give in to the pressure of that place. It'll sneak up on you and devour every last bit. Take the trip, Annie. Greet needs you. And besides, that's what friends do for each other. They show up."

"I don't know Joe," Aunt Peggy said. "Annie doesn't want to leave her fiancé at Christmas, don't be ridiculous."

"Oh, Stewart wouldn't be bothered," he said. "She could scoot down there and be back here before the sleigh lands on our roof."

"Annie, Greet isn't your responsibility," Aunt Peggy said. "You have more obligations than you need right here. Now is not the time to take on Greet's problems. We have a reservation for Christmas Eve dinner. I don't want you to miss that." A knock at the door ended the conversation.

"That should be Stewart," Annie said. "Uncle Joe, he wants to watch the game with you."

She put her pen down and went to the door. Stewart kissed her forehead as he came inside. He carried a platter from the deli around the corner.

"I picked up a charcuterie board for the game," he said.

"Oh, that looks delicious." Annie took his camel hair overcoat and hung it in the closet. They joined Peggy and Joe in the library.

"Ready to watch the Jets dominate?" Stewart said, as he took a seat.

"Let's hope our defensive line can hold them," Uncle Joe replied.

Annie uncovered the dish and placed it on the coffee table. "Let me get some plates and open a bottle of Merlot." She started toward the kitchen then stopped. "What would you all think of playing a game later on? My assistant gave me *Never Have I Ever* as a Christmas gift. It's supposed to be a lot of fun."

"Oh, Annie, I'm too old for such silliness." Aunt Peggy brushed her off.

"Isn't that for kids?" Uncle Joe asked, turning his attention to the television.

"Board games?" Stewart said, picking up a block of cheese. "Who are you and what have you done with Annie? I'll tell you what, we'll go for a walk in the park during half time."

In the kitchen, Annie found four appetizer plates and linen napkins. She searched a drawer and found a wine key. "Walk in the park." She grumbled to herself while perusing the labels in the wine rack. "Doesn't he know it's freezing out there?" She pulled a bottle, and imagining her assistant laughing and cutting up with her friends, cranked the screw into the cork. What had she called them? "Her tribe." The word left a taste of jealousy on her tongue. She levered the key against the bottle and imagined being part of a group like that. "Who am I kidding?" The truth was, she would first have to find the time to make some friends.

Annie was a senior in high school when she moved to Manhattan. The new girl in town. At the time the changes in her life had left her spinning. She'd just lost her mother and was whisked away from her home by her aunt and uncle. Looking back, she wondered if she had been suffering mild depression. Who wouldn't have seen that coming, given all the hits she'd taken.

Her days at school passed in a blur. Thinking back, she could remember her teachers and the text she studied, but she'd be hard pressed to imagine the face of one of her classmates. She never bothered to reach out to the other students and was quite contented to simply be left alone. Focusing on her studies and making her aunt and uncle proud helped to crowd out her homesickness and the longing to be on Bonaire again.

Once she was accepted to NYU, her life continued in a cloud of classes, studying, and her aunt and uncle. At her Aunt Peggy's encouragement, she'd accepted a few dates from some guys in her class, but socializing wasn't something she was interested in. It was a freak happenstance that she'd met Stewart at all.

She pulled the cork from the bottle and tossed it in the trash. Finding her cell, she scrolled, then touched Greet.

Annie: *c u soon*

Greet: *t u*

Chapter Three

Annie was jerked forward and caught by her seatbelt as the plane touched down. She checked the time and was pleased to see they had arrived on Bonaire seven minutes ahead of schedule. Once the plane taxied and came to a complete stop, she fumbled with her woolen winter coat and found the belt's release buckle. As she watched the ground crew push a set of rolling stairs toward the plane, she patted her head and checked that her hair was still smooth and the bun secure. After sliding her bag from under the seat in front of her, she retrieved a second piece that fit neatly into the overhead compartment. Stacking the two, she wheeled them behind her down the narrow aisle. As she grew closer to the exit, warm air rushed in and swamped her in her heavy coat.

Exiting the plane, she stopped at the top of the stairs and without thought, closed her eyes and sucked in a deep breath of salty air. As she exhaled, she opened them and saw the last thing she had seen before leaving the island as a seventeen-year-old. The airport was still a vibrant flamingo pink. She hadn't thought of the unusual shade in years. Perhaps because it never occurred to her that the color was so unique. Now that she had traveled through most of Europe, she could appreciate the idiosyncrasy of it.

Her stomach turned as the warm breeze reached her. She was back on Bonaire. It was easy to let the happy memories flow; shenanigans with her friends, a mother who was more like a buddy, and her father. Her feelings for him were mixed. He'd always called her his best mate, and she whole heartedly returned the sentiment. But the memories of her mother's illness and subsequent death were strong. It seemed the entire island attended her funeral. How many faces stopped and told her what a loss Rose was, to not only her family, but the entire community? And how could someone so easily let their best mate down?

"Excuse me," a man behind her said. "Do you need help with those?" He gestured to her bags.

"No, thank you. I've got it." She was holding up the line and quickly gathered her things. Wearing heels and carrying her luggage, she cautiously descended the aluminum steps. As her foot touched the ground, she heard a familiar voice call out.

"You're actually here." Greet said, approaching her. She wrapped Annie in a hug and spoke into her neck, "I've been dreaming of this day for ten years."

"Greet, it's—" Annie searched for words but they stuck in her throat. She was happy to see her best friend, but the sun beat down and she could feel trickles of sweat gathering on her forehead.

"Thank you so much for coming. It means the world to me to have you here."

Greet's brown eyes were teary and had half moon shadows underneath. Her complexion was pale, her dark hair pushed haphazardly behind her ears. The carefree smile Annie remembered was only a forced grin.

"I always imagined I'd come back," Annie said. "I never thought it would take me so long."

"Look at you." Greet took the luggage and examined the pantsuit and shoes showing from under her coat. "So professional. A big city banker now. I remember when we both dreamed of being teachers. We were going to work and live together forever."

"It sounded nice at the time."

"It sure did." She gazed at her friend. "Follow me, I'm parked out front. And you might want to take off that coat. It's eighty-five degrees out here."

The drive from the airport to Kralendijk, the island's capital, took less than ten minutes. From the passengers' seat, Annie watched the Christmas decorations pass as they traveled along the main street. Like a pastel rainbow, business fronts alternated from pale peach to seafoam green, to an overly cheerful yellow. Palm trees lined the road with strings of white lights circling their trunks. Evergreen wreaths hung equally spaced on the lamp posts and electric candles adorned many of the shops' windows.

"I remember all of this," she said. "It hasn't changed a bit. Does Valentina still—"

"Give out free peppermint ice cream on the 26th? Yep, she sure does."

"Valentina always said it was to help with the post-holiday blues. I think it actually worked. All the gifts had been opened and the holiday was done, I remember looking forward to that ice cream."

Greet slowed the car and they pulled into her driveway. "Home sweet home."

"Thank you for your hospitality," Annie said, as they walked the path to the front door. "I'd be happy to get a room at the hotel if that's easier. I don't want to be an inconvenience."

"No way. This house is already too quiet with Puck gone." She put her palm on her forehead then drug it back over her head. It was then that Annie saw the stress and pain she was trying hard to hide. Her door had an evergreen wreath with shiny holly berries peeking out, but the joyful decoration did little to raise the owner's spirit. She pushed the door open. "Plus, Nel's all excited to meet her Aunt Annie."

"Aunt? Really?"

"Of course. We're practically sisters." She paused and her shoulders fell. "Is that too presumptuous? We were at one time. I guess I thought—"

"That's fine. We *are* like sisters." Annie hoped her friend couldn't hear the doubt in her voice. Phone calls and text messages were one thing, but had they really remained as close as Annie had let on?

"You can hang your coat in this closet," she nodded at a door, "then make yourself at home. I'll take your things upstairs. I've got the guest room set up for you, cleared some space in the closet and emptied a drawer."

"Thank you, I'm sure it'll be fine."

After putting away her heavy wool, Annie looked around the unfamiliar surroundings and was drawn to a narrow console table covered in framed photos. One was decorated with, *Happy Mother's Day,* written in a child's hand at the top. A girl cheesed for the camera and made the shape of a heart with her fingers. This must be Nel. She had her mother's hair and her father's eyes. Annie saw her old friend Puck, the girl's dad, smiling back at her as she studied the young one. She lifted another, with a picture that she recognized, and moved it closer. Familiar smiling faces standing on a beach. She remembered having this exact picture in her home as a child. Her parents had displayed it on the fireplace mantle.

In the image, Greet's mom laughed from on top of her husband Lee's shoulders. Her hands held over her head, fingers forever in a motionless peace sign. Next to them, Annie's father cradled her mother in his arms. Her head was tossed back and toes were pointed. Behind them waves frozen in time crashed to the shore.

She replaced it and picked up another. This one again of four friends near the shoreline, a turquoise sky their backdrop. Only this photo was of Greet, and her future husband, Puck. Annie stood beside them in her swimsuit with a gold metal hung around her neck. Next to her, a boy held Annie's hand high above their heads signaling victory. His white teeth leapt off the picture and his dark hair was a tangled mess after coming out of the water.

"Menno," Annie whispered. She placed her finger on the man's dark mane.

"I always loved that one of the four of us." Greet's comment made her jump. "I'm sorry, you were lost in thought. I didn't mean to scare you. That was the day you won the swim to Klein race. Remember how Menno, Puck and I rowed in kayaks alongside of you?"

"You cheered so loudly I could hear you below the water." She returned the frame to the table top. "Do they still hold that contest?"

"You better believe they do. It grows more popular each year. We just celebrated the 20th anniversary. I think they had almost seven hundred people."

"That many? I'd never win with that much competition, but it's nice to know the race is still going."

"Why don't you run upstairs and change out of that suit? Your bags are in the second bedroom on the left. I thought today we could spend some girl time in town. I'll need to pick up Nel at her school at two o'clock. We'll have plenty of time to catch up."

"Sounds like fun." Annie headed toward the stairs and then stopped. "Greet, I know I'm here because of what you and Puck are going through. I can see how upset you are, it's written all over your face. Your beautiful eyes have lost the sparkle I remember."

"I'm sorry. I'm going to try and not be a total downer while you're here."

"All I'm saying is, please don't feel obligated to entertain me. I really would be just as happy staying here and talking."

"I appreciate that, but let's save the grief and tears for later. I don't want to send you running back to Manhattan your very first day."

―――

The guest room was the color of gooseberries and had a queen-sized bed and a frilly comforter. Ocean and island themed artwork covered the walls. On the nightstand was a tall reading lamp and a dozen or more sea shells. Annie slid them to the side and put her current novel next to the light. She allowed herself one hour per night to read purely for entertainment, a small reward for all the hard reading she did most days. An unfamiliar feeling swept through her when she remembered she was officially on vacation and could read whenever, and for however long, she wanted. Work was on hold for now, and the pure joy of knowing she had free time left her feeling thrilled.

She brushed lint off her shoulder and took a minute to hang her clothes in the closet that Greet had cleared for her. She tucked her other items in an empty drawer and placed her toiletries bag on the dresser. Looking in the mirror, she noticed her hair had worked its way loose, a strand was flying about her head, surely the result of all the travel she had done today. Finding her brush, in no time at all she had it smoothed and the bun neatly secured behind her neck. Greet had suggested she change, but the other outfits she brought were similar to what she already had on. Her stomach rumbled and she checked the time. She grabbed her purse and went downstairs.

"Settled in?" Greet asked. "Let me know if you need anything at all."

"Any chance we can grab lunch soon? I usually have breakfast but only had time for a quick coffee at the airport this morning."

"How does the Bon Air Café sound?"

"Really? It's still open? I can't believe it. It seems like nothing's changed since I left."

The sky was clear and the sun shone down as they walked into town. They passed rows of homes with Christmas trees displayed on the front porches. Most houses on the island were modest in size and a cumbersome six foot evergreen indoors would get in the way of day-to-day life. Leaving the decorated plants outdoors for all to enjoy was a local tradition.

It was an easy walk to the restaurant and soon they were waiting to be seated. The dining room was lined with shiny teal booths and slick veneered tabletops. The lime green and white checkerboard floor reflected the sunlight pouring in the front windows. In the corner, next to the lunch counter, was a tall tree with flashing pink and green lights. A silver star blinking at the apex. The Bon Air Café had its own interpretation of holiday embellishments. Decorative neon tube lights hung on the walls. Greet and Annie were shown to a booth where a parrot, lit up in bright green, looked over them. Annie perused the menu but Greet had it memorized.

"Hey, Greet," a cheerful server welcomed them. "What can I get you for?"

"Hi Corrie." Greet raised her eyebrows. "See anyone you might remember?"

The server squinted and took a closer look at the stranger in the pantsuit. "Sweet baby Jesus. Annie Martis, is that really you?"

Hearing her name, Annie looked up and studied the waitress. "Corrie?"

"Yes, Corrie. Come here, stranger." The enthusiastic friend launched herself at Annie and held her in a vice. "I can't believe you're back. We've been waiting for you forever."

Corrie's grip was strong and her dark curls tickled Annie's nose. Her menu was crushed against her and the table's edge and she waited to be released. When her old friend finally let go, Annie put her hand to her hair and patted it down.

"Corrie, this is an unexpected surprise. It's so good to see you again," Annie said, examining the waitress outfit. "You work here?"

"Yup, living the dream." Corrie scooted in next to Greet. "How long are you staying? We need to get together." A heavy hand landed on a bell in the kitchen. "Joey!" Corrie called across the restaurant. "Your burger's ready. Do me a favor and go pick it up." She looked at her friends and sensed today wasn't a celebration. "Oh, I get it. You're here because Puck walked out on her. I offered to slash his tires but Greet wouldn't hear of it. I got a million ways to get even with that deadbeat." She lowered her voice. "We'll talk privately when Greet's not here."

"You do realize I can hear you," Greet said. "I'm sitting right here."

"Do you still live in New York City?" Corrie asked.

"Yes, I do. Manhattan."

"We always thought you'd come home once you graduated. Then I heard you were staying and taking classes at NYU. What do you do for a job?"

"I'm a banker with Global World."

"No kidding. My sister works at the bank on Kaya Korona Street."

"I'm not a teller, I'm an investment banker." There was no reply, so she explained, "I deal with mergers and acquisitions. Multimillion dollar takeovers, handling of stock and bond transfers and liquidations. I'm on track to be promoted to associate."

"Wow," Corrie said. "That's a lot of big words, good for you. My sister basically makes change. She uses a pocket calculator to make sure she gets the numbers right. I always knew you were something special. I guess everything happened for a reason. Bonaire was just too small for you."

Annie's cell vibrated and she checked the screen. Her boss was calling. "Excuse me." She touched Accept. "Richard, what's up?" She listened for a moment and began shaking her head. "There is no way those numbers are wrong, I double checked them personally. They obviously don't know how to interpret the reports."

Corrie danced her eyebrows at Greet who shrugged her shoulders.

"Please email me the latest spreadsheets." Annie said. "I'll take a look at them and see if there's any discrepancy. No, no problem at all, I'm just having lunch. Call me anytime, this has to be perfect. There's too much riding on this to fail. Thanks Richard, and no need to worry. I'll get this straightened out."

Corrie stood and held her pen and pad. "Greet, I know you'll want the chicken salad."

"No, not today." She tried to smile but only produced a strained grin. "My appetite has been way off. I'll have tea and toast."

Corrie turned to Annie. "What can I get for the boss lady? Lunch is on me."

"Do you have a kale salad with a splash of Modena balsamic?"

"No, but I can get pretty close."

———

After finishing their lunches at the café, Annie and Greet strolled down Kaya Grandi, the main road through town. Cute gift and sweet shops lined the narrow lane. Tourists with brightly colored clothing and sunburned cheeks carried shopping bags filled with their purchases. They stopped and peered in windows then decided to go inside.

"I'd love to pick up some gifts for my aunt and uncle while I'm here." Annie said. "Maybe something unique to the island." They took a minute to admire the treats the bakery had put on display. The store's large front glass was decorated with fake snow and holly branches were hand drawn in each corner. Creampuffs bursting with sugary filling and topped with milk chocolate tempted them to go in. Having just eaten, Annie made a mental note to return at another time.

Ocean Tales, the bookstore, had a sign in the window that read *Meet the Author*. A line of fans was forming along the sidewalk, many of whom held copies of the book. They stepped into the street to easily maneuver around the crowd. A cute art gallery caught Annie's eye.

"May we stop in here?"

"Yes, we may." Greet poked fun at the proper language but Annie didn't notice.

They walked into a shop called *Grey Skies*. Photographs taken around the island covered the walls. Annie stopped and studied one particular framed image. The Willemstoren lighthouse stood on the south shore and the photographer had captured it at sunset. The sky was on fire and the beacon stood strong in front of the glowing red and orange horizon.

Annie stared at the white pillar with four red vertical lines painted around it. At the very top the widow's walk encircled the lantern room. Memories of the lighthouse she had visited countless times as a kid rushed over her.

When the heat of summer made their small home uncomfortable, her parents grabbed blankets and pillows and they would sleep under the stars at the foot of the old structure. Her father would start a fire exclusively for marshmallows as her mother told stories of the keeper's home that was now in ruins near the site. As the evening grew late, Annie would sit in her father's lap and try not to give in to the sound of the rolling waves threatening to put her to sleep.

As the onshore winds cooled them, and with a tummy full of toasted treats, she laid with her head deep in the pillow. She remembered staring up at the lantern room and counting from one. She knew the light would flicker when she got to nine. If nothing else in her life was guaranteed, she knew she could count on that light flashing on nine.

"Beautiful." Greet studied the picture with her. "How many hours did we spend playing around that lighthouse? We take Nel, well," she stuttered, "Puck and I used to take Nel there." Annie held her friend's hand. "I hope one day she'll recall those times."

"I remember camping under the light with my mom and dad. We'd wake with the sunrise and splash in the ocean before heading back home. It seems like a dream now. I was in an extraordinary world back then."

"Same world Annie, just a different time."

"Let me know if you need help with anything." A brunette woman with bright eyes called from behind the register.

"Thank you, I'd—" Annie almost told the woman she wanted to purchase the photograph. She could hang it in her downstairs apartment. But as she studied it further, the melancholy she felt bored deep. Having it at her place would be too painful. She would have to face the memories each day. "I'm still looking." She walked away from the photo and searched through other items. She found a Christmas ornament made from a dried gourd. It had a colorful underwater scene hand-painted on it. She studied the fish and coral and tried to remember their names.

"That's a juvenile yellow tailed damselfish." The shop owner stood next to her and pointed at the image. "And that's blade fire coral, its favorite home."

"Oh, yes, thank you," Annie said. "I used to know all the fish and the different coral on the reef." She found herself agitated at her inability to remember the names. Perhaps her brain was too crammed full of work and numbers to leave space for anything else. She held it up and tried to imagine it hanging next to the crystal bobbles on Aunt Peggy's tree. She placed it back on the shelf.

After perusing through two other stores, it was nearing two o'clock and time to collect Nel from school. They left the shops and walked toward the center of town. Annie stopped in her tracks when they reached the town square. She held out her arms and looked skyward. They had walked into an actual snow storm. Flakes were falling from above and the once green park was now a frozen tundra.

"Look!" Greet said. "It's snowing in the Caribbean!"

Stores had placed snow making machines on their roofs and side-walks. Several inches of the icy flakes had accumulated on the ground and surrounding vegetation. A snow-loving golden retriever rolled on its back and wiggled into the covered grass. It jumped up, snatched its tennis ball, and ran toward them. It dropped the toy at Greet's feet and backed away, tail wagging.

"Hey, Ginger." Greet picked it up. "Okay girl, but just this once." She put everything she had into the throw, but the ball only traveled a few feet before plumping down in the snow. Ginger returned and tried her luck with Annie.

"Okay dog," Annie said. "Get ready." She cocked her arm and launched it, only to have it fall short. Ginger fetched the ball and ran off toward a young couple walking along the park. "These businesses go out of their way to make this nasty stuff?" Annie asked. "You can have it. Snow is cold and slippery and it only takes a few inches to throw New York into complete gridlock. Do you know how difficult it is to get any work done when the subway system is shut down?"

"Oh, bah humbug," Greet said. "Where's your Christmas spirit? Everything's blanketed in fluffy white cotton. It looks so beautiful."

Annie grumbled and Greet grinned as they left their footprints on the sidewalk. They circled the park in the center of town. They hadn't gotten far when Annie stopped and stared up at a ghost from her past. San Bernardo's Church was as tall and as welcoming as she remembered. Constructed in the late nineteen forties, the old yellow and white building still appeared crisp and fresh against the clear sky. The doors were adorned with evergreens and purple bows. Strings of garland ran along the windows on either side.

Snow fell on her as she recalled celebrating faith and community here. It was in this building where she was surrounded by people she loved, and who in turn, loved her. Now the strongest memory of the church was that of her mother's funeral. The pipe organ's once uplifting music had turned grim as the coffin was carried between the pews. That was the last time she stepped foot in her childhood place of worship.

"Father O'Brian!" Greet called to the collared man coming out the door. "Look whose visiting."

The priest approached and removed his glasses.

"Do you remember Annie?" Greet asked.

"I'd never forget one of my parish family," he said. "Annie, look at you. You've finally returned to us. I always hoped you would."

"It's so nice to see you, Father O'Brian. What a pleasant surprise." She smiled at the man who was so instrumental in her upbringing. Sunday school lessons and an active youth group. He was as much a part of San Bernardo as the walls that held the roof aloft. "I haven't exactly returned. I'm only visiting a couple of days."

"I'm glad you've decided to come. It shows real strength to face the memories of

one's past." He placed his hand on her shoulder. "When you moved away, I worried whether you received any grief counseling. I'd planned to meet with you and work with you after your mother left us. Silly me, I thought we'd have all the time in the world to talk and try to understand God's plan." He motioned toward the doors. "Would you like to come inside?"

"No, thank you." The words spilled out. "We're on our way to pick up Nel from school."

"Well, in that case, I'll shamelessly take this time to tell you both I'm looking for volunteers. I need help getting the church hall decorated before the community dinner. Shall I put your names down?"

"I'm not available to volunteer at this time," Annie spluttered. "But I'd be glad to make a financial contribution."

The three stood in uncomfortable silence. Annie was sure she saw the spirit drain from the man in front of her. Was it something she'd said?

"Father," Greet said. "I'd be glad to help. In fact, I stored some things in my attic from lasts year's celebration. I'll be sure to bring them."

"Thank you, Greet." He nodded at them. "Annie." And turned away.

The snowfall ended as they walked out of the square. They arrived at the elementary school right on time for dismissal. A bell rang and children spilled out of the building and ran to waiting parents.

"There she is," Greet said, waving her arm in the air. "Nel!"

Eight-year-old Nel wore a backpack that was almost as big as she was. Her pig tails jumped as she trotted to her mother. "Hi mom." They exchanged a hug and she looked up at the stranger. "Is this my Aunt Annie?"

"Nel, this is Annie Martis. Annie, this is my daughter, Nel."

The two sized each other up. Annie not sure what to make of a child and the young one sensing the unease.

"You like pink." Annie stated the obvious. Nel was covered in it from the bows in her hair down to her sandals.

"You don't."

"You're very perceptive."

"I don't know what that means, but I'm sensing you're right."

Greet looked from her daughter to her friend and back again. She put her hand on her forehead then drug it over her head. "Are you two, okay?"

"Perfect," Annie said.

"We're great mom," Nel added, and took her mother's hand. She loud whispered, "Why is she wearing that? Isn't pants and a jacket too hot?"

On the way home they stopped in the grocery where Greet wanted to purchase ingredients to make gingerbread. The annual contest would be held the night of the church dinner and Nel wanted to enter a house. With all the needed supplies in the cart, they waited in line at the checkout.

"What about the decorations?" Annie asked. "You know, a gumdrop roof and candy cane door. The judges might give extra points if we, Nel, uses some shaved coconut for a snowy yard."

"Oh, mom, she's right." Nel clapped her hands. "We need to make it the best one."

They left the line and pushed the wagon up and down the aisles again. Once they found the additional items, they returned to the register.

"Aunt Annie, will you help me?" Nel asked. "I want to make a princess castle not just a house."

"I like how you think outside the box," Annie said. "Everyone else will have simple little structures. Wait until they see your palace. Blue ribbon here we come. We're going to need licorice strings for the drawbridge. I'll be right back."

Chapter Four

"I can't believe you remembered," Annie said, sitting at the table in Greet's kitchen. "My favorite meal, hamburgers with grape jelly." She took a big bite, closed her eyes, and spoke with a mouth full, "Mmm, this is so good."

"No grape jelly in New York City?" Greet asked. "I knew it was a podunk town. I hope you don't mind if Nel and I stick with the more traditional ketchup."

"No mom, I want the jelly."

"Smart kid." Annie dabbed her napkin on her lip. "Thank you, Greet. I haven't had this since," she thought a moment. "Well, let's just say the last time I put preserves on a burger I was still living on Bonaire."

"Do you have a husband?" Nel had noticed the engagement ring.

"Not yet, but I'm getting married soon." She looked at her finger. "Stewart gave me this ring when he asked me to be his wife."

"Are you going to wear a big dress?"

"I don't know yet. I have three different styles on hold. It's so hard to decide." She took a sip from her glass. "Nothing really screamed out at me as my," she made air quotes, "dream dress."

She had watched marathon episodes of a series where future brides tried on bridal gowns surrounded by besties and moms. The show always ended with the girl overcome with tears of happiness having found just the right one. Annie had given up on the idea of finding a dress that left her in joyful tears.

"I'm sure one of them will do just fine. I'm going to try them all on again when I get home." She made a mental note to call Barbara at the shop to schedule that.

"Is he a prince?"

"Nel," Greet huffed. "That's enough with the third degree. Annie, your ring is gorgeous. Congratulations. Stewart's a lucky man. You haven't told me much about him. Maybe while you're here you can catch me up."

After dinner, Annie volunteered to help with dishes, but her hostess would have none of it. Nel was sent upstairs for a bath and Annie took advantage of the free time.

"Greet, do you mind if I set up my laptop? My boss asked me to confirm some figures."

"Go right ahead," Greet said. "Make yourself at home here." She dug through a kitchen drawer and found the WIFI password scribbled on a piece of paper.

Annie sat on the sofa in the front room with her nose glued to her screen. She pointed and clicked and flew through the document. She frantically hit the buttons on the printing calculator she placed on the coffee table next to her. A full hour had passed when she finally accomplished what she needed to.

"Hello? Anyone home?" Corrie let herself in. She hefted a bottle of wine in her hand and smiled at Annie on the sofa. "I know Greet's a beer drinker, but I've got the fancy boss-lady pegged for an Italian Merlot."

"That sounds perfect right now," Annie said. "Thank you."

While Corrie found wine glasses, Annie sent an email with an attachment back to Richard. She closed her laptop and joined Corrie in the kitchen.

"Corrie, I didn't hear you come in," Greet said, as she and Nel came down the stairs. "Nel, time for bed, sweetheart."

"It's only eight o'clock," the young girl whined.

"Why don't you read a bit?"

"You just wanna have grownup time and I'm too young." She kissed her mother goodnight. "I know, brush my teeth," she said, as she tromped back upstairs.

"Thanks for bringing the wine." Greet said. "Let's sit in the front room. I'll start a fire to chase away this chill in the air."

Corrie poured and passed glasses. Annie sunk into a comfortable arm chair and Corrie snuggled under a blanket on the love seat. Greet snapped twigs into small pieces and laid them across the grate. She tore newspaper and balled it up, then pushed it underneath. She found a book of matches on the mantle and struck one. As the blaze grew, she added thicker twigs and as the fire consumed them, she placed two logs from the hearth on top.

"That should do it." She propped herself on the sofa. They listened as the wood snapped and crackled, filling the room with that comforting aroma that only came from a fire made with love.

"This is so nice," Corrie said. "Thanks for inviting me."

"You're a nut." Greet grinned. "Since when do you need an invitation?"

"Since you and Annie ditched me that time and went hiking up in Karpata without me."

"I'm sorry we hurt your feelings," Greet said. "But that was fifteen years ago. Please, let it go."

"Never," Corrie said. "The hurt is real."

The three enjoyed the fire in easy silence. Annie and Greet growing tired from the long day. Corrie tried her wine and puckered, then she had another taste. Annie took a sip and closed her eyes as the earthy tannins washed over her tongue.

"The way I see it," Corrie said, "We can either draw straws or one of you can volunteer to go first."

"Go first?" Annie asked.

"Isn't that why we're here? To work through the messes that are currently your lives?"

"My life isn't a mess," Annie said.

"We'll see about that." Corrie countered.

"Ugh, okay, we can start with me." Greet straightened. "I'll admit, things are in chaos. My husband, who I love very much, left me and our daughter." She paused. "Saying those words sounds so strange to me. I never once thought I'd end up being a single parent, but here I am."

"Damned that Puck," Corrie said. "I hope his man parts fall off."

"With Christmas just around the corner," Greet continued, "being alone is really tearing me up. I'm struggling to hide it from Nel, but I'm feeling no holiday spirit. She's so young and I don't want my problems to become hers." She pulled the quilt off the back of the couch, draping it over her legs and feet. "I keep reassuring her and telling her everything is going to work out. I don't know what to do." Her eyes went glassy. "I love Puck. I always have."

"What happened to you two?" Annie asked. "I'm sorry to be so forward, but you've been together since we were teens. I remember when he asked you out on your first date. I think we were in our freshman year of high school."

"We were so excited for you," Corrie said. "Annie and I showed up at your house to help you get ready. Do you remember that? How long did it take to decide on your outfit?"

"That was such a fun night." Annie surprised herself when she clearly recalled the event. "You would've thought he'd asked out all three of us. We wanted you to wear your hair down but you insisted on a ponytail."

"I wanted you to wear my little black dress, but you wore jeans." Corrie smiled. "Had I known he was taking you to Tina's Gelato Shop, I never would've pushed so hard on the blasphemous look."

"Dating and high school was one thing," Greet said. "Me getting pregnant our senior year was a reality check. Looking back—" A tear trickled down her cheek. "I don't think he ever really wanted to marry me. I imagine his parents told him he had to do the right thing."

Annie found Kleenex and joined her friend on the sofa. She snapped out two and handed them to her.

"I don't get it," Corrie said. "You've always been happily married. Why now? Why did Puck move out now?"

"Over the last year," Greet said, holding tissues to her nose, "I watched all the happiness drain out of him. It happened right before my eyes. He became quiet and only talked about building up hours on his paycheck." She sniffled. "Money has always been tight, but I never minded going without. I thought he felt the same way. He wanted to be at work more than he wanted to be home with us. I couldn't stand to see him so miserable and to know I was the one causing it. When he said he was going to move out, I just let him go."

"Did you two ever talk about this?" Annie asked. "I mean, about being happy with the way things were."

"Sure, we did. But then my car would need a repair and he'd have to give up his Saturday and pick up an extra shift. I guess he just got tired of trying to take care of us and found someone who would take him as is."

"You think there's another woman?" Corrie asked.

"It sure seems that way." She dabbed her eyes with her now drenched tissue.

"That no-count whore," Corrie said. "We need to find out who she is."

"What good is that going to do?" Annie asked, handing Greet a fresh Kleenex.

"Once we know, it's mission sabotage." The comment was met with silence. "Haven't you guys seen *Parent Trap*? The camping scene? It's a classic." When she only got confused looks, she added, "Just leave it to me."

"I appreciate your support Corrie, but he's a grown man." Greet mused, "It was the strangest thing. The sadder he grew the more my own happiness dwindled. We became like two zombies only putting on our human skin when we were with Nel."

Annie opened her arms and Greet fell into her embrace. She laid her head in the crook of her neck and began to sob.

"I love him," she said, through tears. "What will I do without him? Last week he called me. He wanted to set up a time to pick up Nel for movie night. When we started to say good-bye, I said, 'Love you, Big Duck.' It's my silly nickname for him. We've been saying I love you before we hang up for so many years, it just slipped out." She grabbed more tissues and blew her red nose. "Obviously, he went dead silent. Probably thinks I'm off my rocker. The hardest part is, I do love him. I want him back, for Nel and for me."

"We're going to need more alcohol." Corrie picked up Annie's empty glass and disappeared into the kitchen.

Greet's weeping quieted and she moved away from Annie. "I'm sorry." She straightened. "Oh no, I think I got tears on your blouse. Why don't you give that to me?" She started to get up. "I've got a bleach pen in the—"

"Don't you dare. Sit back down here." She patted the cushion. They listened as Corrie rattled around in the kitchen. Annie fixed the quilt so it covered them both.

"I wish..." Annie stumbled over her words. She couldn't promise to be here for her friend, she'd be returning to Manhattan soon. She knew she was expected to reassure her and tell her that everything was going to be alright, but how did she know? Had she jumped in right on time to watch the end of her best friend's marriage? After she popped out of her life again, Greet would be left to carry on without her, just as before. Nothing would have changed.

"Do you remember when—" Annie's phone buzzed. "I'm sorry." She stood and all the warmth from under the blanket escaped. "Richard, hello. Did you get the document?" Annie looked at her distraught friend, eyes red. "I sent an attachment explaining the area that's causing this confusion. Hold on, let me get online. We'll go over it together." She mouthed *sorry* to her friends and disappeared into the kitchen with her laptop.

"Well, that's totally rude," Corrie said, returning to the room.

"She can't help it," Greet said. "She's, she's—"

"Not the friend we used to know."

"That's not true. Annie just has a very important job."

Having placed two more logs on the fire, they talked among themselves and Corrie finished her wine. Half an hour later, Annie rejoined them.

"My deepest apologies. Trying to avoid a mushroom cloud at the bank." She sat next to Greet as Corrie got up and disappeared into the kitchen.

"I hope everything's okay." Greet said, making room for Annie under the blanket.

"From your lips to God's ears. The client is having a hard time following the math. I'm afraid I have some work to do in the morning. I need our clients to clearly understand the proposal."

Annie needed to get this marriage back together. Coming to Bonaire was a mistake. She had a lot of work to do and the clock was ticking. Fix Greet's marriage and be back in Manhattan as soon as possible. That was the new plan.

Corrie returned with mugs of hot chocolate and placed them on the tables. "I spilled a little coffee liqueur in them." She then used the poker on the fire, springing it back to life, and tossed a pillow on the floor. She sat down in front of the revived blaze.

"Do you remember when my mom got her diagnosis?" Annie asked.

"Oh, Annie," Greet said. "Of course we do, I'll never forget that horrible day. I went to your house after school. We were going to teach ourselves that new line dance. Your mom was as pale as an angel's wing. Looking back, the cancer was already stealing her away, we just didn't know it yet. She told me you'd stormed out after hearing the diagnosis and didn't know where you'd gone."

"I've always wondered," Annie said. "If they'd caught it earlier, would she still be alive?"

"I left your house and high-tailed it to find you. I knew you'd be at the lighthouse, there was never any doubt."

"Once you found me there, do you remember what you told me?" Annie asked.

"I said it felt like I was losing my own mom, and that you weren't going to go through this alone."

"I've never forgotten those words. I can't tell you how much that meant to me. We're sisters, and I won't stand by and watch your marriage crumble."

Chapter Five

"I cannot believe I'm having to do this in the Caribbean." Annie grumbled to herself as she slowed to a jog and carefully moved over the snow-covered sidewalk. The army of machines ran constantly and the accumulation in the park was approaching a foot. As she neared San Bernardo, she cut left and swung around the back of the church where the streets were sleet-free. She picked up her pace. It was early morning and she had snuck quietly out of the house just as the sun was making its appearance. There were no cars to be seen, so she traveled down the center lane. When she knew she had passed the blocks of snow, she turned again and ran toward the coastline. As the ocean came into view, she was momentarily startled by its beauty and fell to a walk. A gentle breeze traveled onshore and brought with it the briny promise of another beautiful day. She huffed, hands on hips, as she neared the white beach sparkling in the sunlight. The coral crunched underfoot as she approached the water. The sea was so clear she could see colorful fish swimming just a few feet from her.

"You look like a queen triggerfish." She squinted in the sunlight and peered closer into the surf. "I remember you. Let me see who else is there." The abundance of sea life tested her memory. "A trunk fish, a yellow tang." Her voice, that of a child's. "Look at all those butterfly fish." A strong wave rushed toward her and she shuffled backward. "Oh no you don't, these running shoes are leather Prada's."

After saving her footwear from the salty water, she returned to the quiet road and continued her run. Sweat dotted her forehead and her leg muscles grew tight. She made the turn for home and completed her targeted three miles. Stretching her arms over head and twisting at her waist, she cooled down as she walked back to the house. The change of scenery had taken her mind off work, but as the home came into view, she thought about last night's call from Richard. They'd spent some time going over terms and agreements. This morning, she had to recheck figures and take a look at how the stock market opened.

"Nel, if you'll let me finish my coffee, you'll get to work with a happy Aunt Annie and not the Grinch." Annie sat at the kitchen table with her laptop open in front of her. Having showered and dressed after the run, she was following up with her boss regarding the questions he had the previous night. She wore a fitted navy dress with a cropped blazer, heels, and her hair was tightly twisted into its bun. A steaming full mug sat beside her.

"Are you sure the two of you are going to be okay today?" Greet placed a bowl of cereal in front of her daughter. "I should be done at the salon around three o'clock. Then we can go do something fun." She topped off her travel mug.

"Can we go frog hunting?" Milk dripped off Nel's spoon.

"No, not today."

"So, by fun, you mean boring."

Greet kissed her daughter on her cheek. "I can't wait to see your palace when I get home. We have to have it in the church hall before seven o'clock to be eligible for the competition."

"I don't care about the contest," Nel said. "I just want to make it *so* beautiful."

"What?" That got Annie's attention. "Of course, we... you, want to win. Otherwise, what's the point in entering?"

"Annie," Greet said. "The idea is for the kids to have fun."

"Right, have fun *winning*." She returned her attention to the computer and splayed her fingers across the keyboard. "Do you think the salon would have a manicure appointment available today? My nails are a hot mess."

"Me too, mom. Mine are hot too."

"I'm sure we'll have something open. I'll check the schedule when I get there and shoot you a text." Greet called from the front door, "Have fun. Stay out of trouble."

When all the flakes were gone, Nel dropped her bowl into the sink and waited patiently in front of the television. It took Annie over an hour, but she was confident she had found the accounting in question and could easily explain the perceived discrepancy to Richard. After typing up a lengthy clarification, she hit Send and closed her laptop. Annie put her mug and Nel's bowl in the dishwasher and went to find the girl in the front room.

"Thanks for letting me get that work done," Annie said. "Ready to start our project?"

"Yes!" Nel clicked off the TV and joined Annie in the kitchen. "I think we're going to make a good gingerbread team."

"We have all the ingredients to make the dough." She lined them up on the counter then found a large bowl and mixer. "Still planning on the castle design?"

"Yup, I know we can do it."

"Okay then. We'll need a lot of cardboard to create the template. A box cutter, an exacto knife, ruler, and heavy tape." She searched in several drawers. "I really should write all this down. Does your mom have a rolling pin and piping bags?"

"She keeps them in the pantry." Nel fetched the items and placed them on the counter. "I've got a box we can use for the ten plate. My turtle got so big, I set him free."

"Any chance you have a protractor?"

Nel randomly searched the kitchen. "Nope. No tractor."

"You grab your jacket. I'll borrow your mom's sweatshirt. We'll need to go to town for some things."

———

"Look Aunt Annie! The snow is falling!" Nel took off running down the sidewalk toward the manmade blizzard. The snow machines had been working nonstop and now almost a foot blanketed the town square. Carols played from hidden speakers and an entire Christmas village was set up on the lawn. A towering tree twinkled color lights, just as Annie's tree at home once did. Wooden elves climbed ladders adding decorations to its boughs. Santa's chair, with red quilted cushions and gold trim, sat empty waiting for the jolly old man to arrive there on Christmas Eve. Children were playing in the drifts and had made a good effort creating a snowman.

"Aunt Annie, have you ever made a snow angel?" Out of nowhere a packed ball hit Nel on her cheek and neck. She put her hand to the area and tears started to pool.

"Nel, are you okay?" The spot was covered in ice crystals and already turning red. They searched for the offender. A boy about Nel's age stood grinning at them. His front teeth were missing and his cheeks were rosy.

"You better run Charlie!" Nel made a ball, and carrying it like a professional player, took off after the culprit.

"Nel!" Annie called out. "Are you sure you want to do that?"

The eight-year-old launched it in the perfect trajectory. Charlie's eyes grew wide but his feet wouldn't move in the snow. The ball hit him square in the chest.

"Yes!" Nel threw her hands in the air. "Bullseye!"

Charlie ran off, not interested in getting pelted again.

Annie placed her hand on Nel's shoulder. "Good job. You showed him. I bet he thinks twice before messing around with you again." She searched the square. "Let's go to the general store. I'm sure they'll have some of the things we need." Annie chose her steps carefully, her heels making the trek difficult. Before she made it very far a snowball burst on the back of her head and dripped inside her neckline.

"Wow!" Nel was delighted. "Another perfect shot! I was aiming for your stupid bun." She giggled and started scooping up more.

"So that's the way this is going down." Annie pulled her hoodie over her head and packed a wet mess between her hands. "You better run you little mischief-maker."

Nel's laugh grew uncontrollable as she ran in circles around her aunt. The young girl dodged all of Annie's attempts to even the score. Annie grabbed handfuls and sent some that landed close to her moving target, but none made their mark. Suddenly, a golden retriever appeared and ran back and forth between them. It jumped up and caught flying balls in its mouth only to crush them to pieces and go after the next.

Nel circled closer and Annie tugged her hoodie down around her face. As she attempted to throw another one, the dog grabbed her sweatshirt at the cuff. It pulled on the fabric and brought Annie crashing into the snow.

"Ginger! No!" A man's voice was approaching. "Sit Ginger, sit."

Nel came running to be sure her aunt was okay.

"I'm sorry Greet," the man said. "She snuck out of the store. I guess she really wanted to play in the snow."

"That's not my mom." Nel said as Annie sat in the powder and pushed her hoodie back. "That's my Aunt Annie. Annie Martis."

The man studied the stranger covered in snow. Flakes fell about them, landing on her cheeks and eyelashes.

"Annie," he whispered.

"Menno."

Annie didn't notice the snow that was melting in her shoes and clinging to her bare legs. She knew she was staring but couldn't make herself blink. She'd be lying to herself if she said running into her first love hadn't crossed her mind. But there he stood, holding his hand out to her. She cleared her head and reached up to him. Expecting sparks to shoot from their touch or tingles to run through her body, she was disappointed when neither happened. He pulled her to her feet and she took a few swipes at the snow that stuck to her bottom.

At one time this man was her everything. They became friends while in the first grade. Their shared competitive spirit kept them racing across the playground and later drove one another to excel in academics. Earning the higher score ensured bragging rights for a week. When they entered high school and were put on different tracks, they became acutely aware of the fact that they missed seeing each other. Annie found herself thinking of his kind eyes and the way he raked his hand through his dark hair. They knew these feelings were more than just two friends being separated during the school day. Neither one could tell you when it happened, but somewhere along the way, they had fallen in love.

"Menno, I..." She faltered.

"Annie, what..." He was speechless.

"We're making a gingerbread castle," Nel said. "Aunt Annie and I are a team. We need a tractor and a ruler."

"Protractor," Annie breathed. As if in a dream, staring at the boy she was taken away from at seventeen. She forced herself to blink. "We need a protractor and a ruler." She studied him, unable to look away.

"Don't forget the exact knife," Nel said, as if from a distance.

"Exacto knife," she said with a wisp of air.

"And heavy tape. We got the cardboard at home." Nel added, "You said we need to cut a box."

"Box cutter," Annie shook her head, trying to awaken from this dream. "We need a box cutter."

Menno visibly took a breath and a smile replaced his stare. "Sounds like you've got a big project ahead of you."

"We're making a castle for the gingerbread contest." Nel said. "We got gumdrops for the roof, I only ate a few."

"I should've known it would be a competition that brought you home," Menno said. "Come inside, let's see what we've got."

They followed him into *Dad's General Store*. A Christmas tree sparkled by the entrance. Among its twinkling lights were tags with names written on them. Families in need and their wishes for the holiday. A sign hanging on its branches invited customers to take a name and sponsor the family this Christmas.

"You work here?" She asked as they walked down an aisle. The shop was expansive and held a variety of items. "They've got everything. Clothes, canned goods, hiking shoes."

"And this." He held up a protractor, searched some more, and found a ruler.

Big barrels filled with penny candy formed a circle near the register. Laffy taffy, MaryJane's and Smarties heaped above the rims. Nel found a Sugar Baby and began opening it.

"Nel, no," Annie said. "We'll have to pay for that first."

"We don't pay for the candy," Nel said. "It's free."

"Free? Nel, no—"

"Sure, it's always free for the kids," Menno said. "Makes shopping with mom and dad, or Aunt Annie, less like work and more like fun." He searched a barrel and handed her a chocolate coin in gold foil. "Still like the sweets?"

"Yes, always." She unwrapped the piece and popped it into her mouth. "Oh, that's good."

"Here." He found another treat. "I'll bet you'll like this beauty." He stretched a candy necklace over Annie's head and adjusted it around her neck. "A sweet for the sweet. Although I imagine a set of pearls would me more fitting with that dress." He stared at her until she nervously patted her head and dropped her eyes. "Nel, what were the other items?"

After finding all they needed, Annie stood at the register. Menno put the purchases in a brown bag and Annie opened her wallet.

"On me."

"Are you sure? Thank you." She searched for more to say but only found a lump in her throat. She choked out, "Thank you again." She turned to leave and touched her hair. The snowball had loosened the bun and the hoodie had pulled strands free. She'd have to fix that when they got home.

They rolled the dough into sheets and placed the cardboard cutouts. Nel slid a knife along the edges of the templates. Annie helped to place them on a cookie sheet and soon they spun a revolving door of dough in and out of the oven. The inviting smell of cinnamon and ginger filled the kitchen.

"Nel, these look perfect." Annie inspected the first pieces to bake.

Nel continued working, cutting a long, narrow shape and then adding windows at the top. Annie laid this piece over the rolling pin before putting it in the oven.

"That's going to be one of the turrets. We'll bake it in a curved shape."

Nel created the other three towers in the same way. Once all the pieces were out of the oven, they took a break and made lunch while they waited for everything to cool. Nel took her sandwich into the front room and ate while watching television. Annie sat at the table and fretted. Baking complete, she didn't have a task to keep her hands busy and her mind off of Menno. He was no longer the boy she remembered but had grown into a handsome man. *No, no, no, think of Stewart. Stewart's eyes, his hair.* But it was no use, thoughts and visions of the man she once loved wouldn't leave her.

Before Annie left Bonaire, she and Menno each promised the

other a never-ending love. They swore to wait, hopeful that one day they'd be together again. But when you're seventeen all things seem possible. She wasn't interested in meeting boys, but her Aunt Peggy wouldn't stop dropping hints. When Senior Ball came and went without a date, she saw the disappointment in her aunt's face. Annie begrudgingly began dating.

It was at this time she ended all contact with Menno. Destroying her heart a second time, she ignored his messages and had gone so far as to request that Greet not speak about him. The complete removal of Menno from her life was a desperate coping mechanism. It was the only way she could move on when faced with a path she did not choose.

"All done." Nel put her plate in the sink and touched the gingerbread. "It feels cool. Should I put it together now?"

"Let's do it."

Annie cleared the table then place a sturdy piece of cardboard on it. "Build it on this so we'll be able to carry it to the church."

Nel chose the pieces and began assembling. Annie offered a second pair of hands, holding the parts together while the sticky sugar glue dried. With lots of patience and great determination, the castle steadily grew. When the final cone roof was placed on the last tower, Nel threw her arms in the air and Annie cheered for her.

"You did it!" Annie smiled proudly. "It looks beautiful."

"I'd say it does." Menno walked into the kitchen. "But it isn't the prettiest thing in this room."

"Menno," Annie checked her hair.

"I thought I'd stop by and see how the construction was coming along."

"I did it!" The young girl was giddy. "I made a castle." She gestured toward the sugar covered creation.

"Wow, that looks great," Menno said. "Fit for the Queen."

"Why don't we take a rest and let the paste harden?" Annie said. "Then you can—"

"Decorate it! Can I watch TV again while we wait?"

"I don't know about that. You already watched a bunch today. Do you have a book to read?"

"Daddy built me a library in the corner of my room. It has a huge bean bag chair." Nel climbed the stairs. "Don't decorate without me," she yelled from the second floor. "And don't eat all the gumdrops."

"What a nice surprise." Annie smoothed the front of her already smooth dress.

"Come on Annie," he said. "You actually thought I'd stay away?"

"I didn't know what to think." She blushed. "May I offer you a drink? I think Greet has soda, or I can make a hot tea."

"No thank you," he said. "I was hoping we could talk. Maybe we could catch up a bit."

"I'd like that."

They moved into the front room where Annie sat on the sofa. A flush crept over her when he made himself comfortable beside her. She placed her palm on her hair and patted the perfect locks.

"You look great," he said. "The big city life has been good to you."

"Thank you, it has."

"The last time we spoke, you weren't doing so well. If I remember, you were homesick and still trying to fit in."

"My aunt and uncle helped me a lot," she said. "I can't imagine how difficult it was for a childless couple to take in a teenager they hardly knew."

"I'm sure you weren't difficult. They were lucky to get you. If I had been lucky, they would've left you here."

"Are you sure I can't get you something?"

"No, I'm fine," he said. "I haven't heard from you in years and suddenly you're wrestling with my dog in the square. I'm having a hard time believing it."

"Me too. Greet and I walked through town yesterday," she said. "A lot of things seem just the same, and yet, I feel like a fish out of water. I'm just a visitor now."

"*You've* changed," he said. "So professional and proper. You're wearing heels around the house like its nothing. Do you remember the party we went to when you decided to wear your new shoes?"

"Oh my, yes." She grinned. "Those stilettos lasted about an hour, then I danced the rest of the night barefooted."

"And today you're wearing them without a second thought."

"I guess I have changed." She wiggled her toes. "That would explain why I feel like a stranger in my own hometown." They were washed in an uncomfortable silence. To break the stillness, Annie said, "Tell me about your job at the general store. How long have you been working there?"

"At least you didn't mention the weather." They giggled. "Almost six years. It's a good life. It keeps me in town and in touch with what's going on in Kralendijk. I hate to brag, but I was the first one to know about Mrs. Brookshire's cat getting stuck on her roof."

"Wow, you *are* in touch." She smiled. "A paralegal I work with brings her cat into the office a few days a week. I understand how much trouble they can be. I'm employed by Global World Bank. Our office is on Wall Street. All those times I beat your math test scores really paid off."

"You were always an aficionado with numbers, but I never would've guessed you'd make your living at it." He studied his shoes. "Why did you do it Annie?" He glanced at her from under his brow. "Why did you totally ghost me? You disappeared, fell off the map, and even Greet wouldn't talk about you."

"She was only doing what I asked of her. I'm so sorry. I took the cowards way out."

"You're no one's coward, Annie."

"After keeping in touch with you all those months, I just couldn't do it anymore. I didn't want to be in love with a man I had little chance of ever seeing again."

"But we could've worked something out."

"How? We were kids. My life was in Manhattan and Bonaire seemed so far away. You may as well have been a million miles from me. I was getting used to living in a strange new world."

"We promised each other forever, remember? I was willing to wait for our together."

"Menno, we were so young. I didn't see any other choice, there was no future for us. I'm sorry. If I could do it over I would. I'd be kind and talk to you and help you to understand."

"I had a plan for us." He took her hand. "I was working on a transfer to Columbia University for my sophomore year. We would've been together again."

"W-what?" Annie felt her heart sink. In a blink she imagined all that could have been. "I had no idea. I don't understand, w-why didn't you tell me?"

"I tried." Anger and disappointment filled his eyes. "You didn't take my calls or reach out to me. Greet refused to hear a word I said and—"

"Menno, I had no... I never—"

"It's all water under the bridge now, isn't it? You made a good life for yourself. I'm happy for you." He stood. "Thank you for seeing me." He opened the door then looked back at her. He raised his chin at her ring. "When's the date?"

She studied the diamond she knew had cost five figures. "April. At The Plaza Hotel on Fifth Avenue."

Chapter Six

"Wonderful job, Nel. I have never seen anything like it in my entire life." Annie stood with her hands on her hips and admired the final product. Menno had left her quietly distressed and the contest was a nice distraction. "The princess looking out the window was a great idea."

"She's the one who lives there. Are you going to the church with me?"

"I wouldn't miss it. We're a team."

"Good. I want you to meet my best friend. He always brags because he has three aunts, but at least now I have one. Charlie made a gingerbread house too."

"Snowball Charlie? He's your best friend?"

"Yup. He got me with that throw but I'm gonna win first prize."

The slightly lopsided structure dripped with sugar glue. Nel's tiny fingerprints had somehow been captured in the gingerbread, and the roof sagged under the weight of the gumdrops. An excessive amount of confectioner's sugar rained down like snow. Patches of shaved coconut stuck haphazardly to the cardboard base. The project having been completed, the kitchen itself could only be described as a war zone.

Candy canes that didn't make the final design laid broken, and crushed vanilla wafers covered the counter tops. Green buttercream frosting had dried on the piping tips and was smeared over Nel's mouth and cheeks.

"We better get to work on this mess before our nail appointment," Annie said. "It looks like a pack of Santa's elves had it out in here."

"My mom uses this." She pulled a bottle of spray cleaner from under the sink. Using a lot of elbow grease and a twice over scrubbing, the kitchen was returned to its pre-castle state. Nel changed her splattered clothes for a new shirt and short. Together, they walked to the salon.

The sign above the large front windows read, *Out of this World Hair and Nails.* Annie held the door open and Nel ran inside. The shop was busy with manicurists and stylists primping their customers. Greet held a blow dryer in one hand and a round brush in the other. She pulled and brushed and studied her client's head. Annie couldn't help but notice the stress on her face. Nel skipped to her and wrapped her arms around her mother's waist.

"Hello there," Greet's arms continued to fly. "Ready to get your nails all prettied up?" She looked around for her co-worker who had agreed to tend to the young girl. "Go sit with Becca. She's going to paint your fingers."

Annie waved from the reception area then took a seat. Soon a familiar face approached her. She felt her mouth fall open and her heart begin to pound. Unexpected tears began to pool.

"Orion," she said, breathless. "It's so good to see you."

The seventy something woman had owned this shop since Annie was a child. Her dark hair was now peppered with grey but her makeup was still flawless. She wore a pretty muumuu in a bright flower print and a pair of sport sandals with a thick heel.

"Annie, I knew you'd come back to us," Orion said. "It's like nature making a correction and sending rain after an unfruitful summer." Annie stood and the two women embraced. Orion held her firmly and Annie closed her eyes. She inhaled the warmth and sunshine that naturally rolled off the woman who was once her mother's dear friend. "Come sit with me. We have a lot of catching up to do."

Annie swept at her tears as she followed Orion to her work station. She planted herself in the chair across from her and the manicurist took her hands.

"Go ahead and cry child, let your sadness flow." Orion studied her fingers. She touched a cotton ball to polish remover and rolled it over the tips. Annie couldn't stop her eyes from leaking. "I would've kept you myself if they'd let me. You were born an island girl. They moved a starfish to the land and expected it to flourish. You have saltwater and sand running in your blood. Bonaire island is engrained in every inch of you." Annie sniffled while Orion applied a moisturizer to her hands. "I hear you've done exceptionally well. Of course you would, you were always such a bright child. But you're not on the right path. Your mama married a local boy and made her home here. She intended for you to do the same."

Annie peered through her tears as blurry wrinkled hands massaged hers. The cream was thick, and as Orion worked it into her skin, it warmed and soothed her. Orion's caring words and gentle touch reminded her of her mother. "Don't fight who you are, child. Dark mane and that island complexion. Some things shouldn't be hidden away." She swiftly worked an emery board and smoothed the edges. "So neat and proper, a designer dress and tall heels. But I can feel your beautiful hair being strangled. Nothing in nature can survive under those rules." Searching through a drawer, she found a small bottle and turned it over twice. Her steady hand removed the small brush then smoothed it over her nails. "This pale green, the color of nature, will bring you peace. You need to refresh your soul but it will only happen if you let it." When she finished the second coat, she found another color and a miniature sized brush. On each of Annie's index fingers she painted a bird in flight. "Freedom is what you seek. You don't know it yet, but you need to break the bond that holds you. It's keeping you from true happiness."

Only after she stepped outside of *Out of this World* did her tears stop falling. Nel stayed behind and would walk home with her mother. She promised the young girl they would meet at the house and Annie would help her carry the castle down to the church. After everything Orion had to say, she was glad for the opportunity to spend some time alone.

In spite of the blizzard blowing through the center of town, the sun was shining and the air was warm. She stopped at the corner and held her face to the sky. Rays touched her cheeks and she closed her eyes and felt the warmth grow.

It was December all across the globe, but here the winter months only meant cooler evenings and stronger winds. Bonaire moved between just two seasons, rainy and dry. And although the word could scare away tourists, the wet season rarely saw more than a few inches.

Orion had a lot to say, but Annie wasn't quite ready to process it all. Strangled hair and something about finding freedom. The older woman certainly could be eccentric. She crossed the street and walked the two blocks to the beach. Looking out at the ocean, she remembered countless hours spent at the shore with her parents. Her mother packed lunch and snacks and her dad never hesitated to splash into the ocean with her. Inflatable inner tubes, frisbees and endless games of paddle ball filled her waking hours. She'd inherited her passion for swimming from her father. He was the only one who could ever beat her in a race. Swimming, for fun or competition, was another thing she had left behind when she moved away.

The beach was quiet, she watched as a scuba diving boat zoomed by. Excited divers wore wetsuits and attached gear to a row of air tanks. Annie carried her heels in one hand and stepped into the warm sand. Wiggling her toes, she sank into the soft powder. With each step she took, the sand gently scratched her tired feet. The nearby waves kept time as they reached the shore. Their rhythmic fall pulled her to them like an old friend beckoning. The foamy saltwater crashed then spread over the sand, inching toward her. It swirled around her feet then retreated again, calling to her to follow.

Orion's haunting words were distracting. How could the manicurist have known her mother's intentions for her? What did she mean about fighting who she was? Annie wasn't doing any such thing. A rogue wave rushed in and soaked her up to the hem of her dress. The water was warm and gave a gentle pull as if inviting her to join in its depths. She tossed her shoes to the shore and walked in deeper. *You have saltwater and sand running in your blood. Bonaire island is engrained in every inch of you.* Diving under an approaching wave, she swam out into the crystal-clear water.

Annie laid on the beach and let the sun dry her. Strangely, she didn't care that her tailored dress would never be the same. She remembered learning how to scuba dive with her father when she was still in elementary school. Her mother worried she was too young but her father only rolled his eyes.

"Too young to dive?" Her father had said. "My daughter? She was ready last year. Rose, there's so much for her to see. The ocean will open up another world for her. Diving will anchor her to the earth."

Once she had become a proficient diver, Annie knew her father's greatest joy was exploring the reefs surrounding the island with her. He taught her the different species of fish, the difference between coral and sponges. The quiet times they spent together under the water were some of her happiest memories. With no verbal communication at depth, over time they developed their own hand signals. They appeared to be playing charades as they moved fingers and arms through the water. The day her father signaled, *We have to cut this dive short, your mother needs us to pick up a roast at the butcher,* and Annie understood each word, was the day she knew their relationship was something special.

Sunbeams touching her face, and her dress now almost dry, she closed her eyes and listened to the music of the island. She heard water lapping on the shoreline and seagulls cawing overhead. The onshore breeze, the woodwinds to the melody. The comforting sounds and warm rays lulled her to sleep.

She didn't know how long she'd been dozing when voices from a couple walking the shore woke her. After she swiped at the sand that stuck to her legs, she stood and started down the beach. With each step, she felt somehow lighter, not in weight, but on the inside. Napping on the warm sand under the gentle sun had reenergized her soul. Without giving this rejuvenation any thought, she began to hum. The beautiful day inspired her and soon she was singing the lyrics to *Christmas Island.* She had to hand it to Jimmy Buffett, he sang it better, but it felt so good she began to really belt it out. "Hang your stocking on a swaying palm tree..." She giggled and played air steel drums, "Santa's gonna arrive in a canoe..." The final verse having been sung, like a drowning man surfacing for air, she started over again.

As she approached the town's fishing pier her singing faded. A commercial boat was docked there and unloading the day's catch. She climbed onto the wharf and stood half hidden behind a weather-beaten piling. Three men crewed the boat, each one baked to a leathery brown, no doubt from the long hours spent on the water. One operated a joy stick, maneuvering a crane that lifted nets filled with Dorado and Wahoo. Water poured from it as it swung across the boat's deck and out over the dock. With a click of a lever, it spilled the fish into a sturdy wheeled container. One man held a shovel and threw ice on the fish as they were loaded. He had a peculiar scar across his face that distorted his left eye and nostril. It cut across his misshapen cheek and lip.

She watched the men until the entire catch had been unloaded. Walking back to Greet's house, she would change her clothes and fix her hair, then go back into town. There was someone she needed to see.

———

"Looks like Father O'Brian's prayers are being answered." Annie spoke to herself as she trudged through the snow toward San Bernardo's Church. She was prepared to hang lights and garland and help Father O'Brian with whatever else he needed.

Annie knew this church. She pulled open the heavy door and went inside. She was immediately struck by the familiar smell of furniture oil and incense. The nave was quiet and she couldn't resist taking a look. She had grown up among the congregation here. At one time she could tell you the name of the artist who created the rose window over the alter. She strolled passed the pews studying the stained glass and the eyes that had watched over her during the course of her childhood. Standing in front of the alter, she was overwhelmed by a wave of loneliness. She searched below the communion rail and picked up one of the kneeler cushions. The fine needlepoint had been done by her mother many years ago. A shepherd tending his flock in a field of green. Running her hand over it, she hoped to find comfort. Instead, her melancholy only grew.

"Annie Martis?"

She jumped. She hadn't noticed the man sitting in the front pew. "Puck?"

He stood and grabbed her around the waist. Annie's feet left the floor and he made two complete turns before setting her down again. "Man are you a site for sore eyes. I didn't know you were home."

The word caught her. Home was in Manhattan. She was a visitor here. "Greet invited me. Gosh it's good to see you."

"Well, I'll be damned. Annie's come home." He held her shoulders and studied her face, seemingly to convince himself she was really there. "God, we've missed you. Does Menno know you're here? He's going to bust a gut."

"Yes, I've seen him." She wasn't confident in her ability to discuss the man she once loved. "I was just taking a peek at the church, so many wonderful memories here. What are you doing sitting here all alone?"

"Greet's dropping off decorations after her shift. We stored some at the house since space is limited here."

"So, you're hiding from her?" Annie thought maybe he had been praying for forgiveness. Having run out on his family and the possibility of a woman on the side would certainly warrant it. All actions of a man she recognized but no longer knew.

"If you're going to put it that way, then yes, I'm hiding. Once she's gone, I'm going to help with the decorating."

"I am too. Father O'Brian asked me if I'd lend a hand. But I can sit with you if you'd like." They sat and stared up at the rose window over the alter. The fading sun shone through the colored glass. The rays caught in a dusty haze like a ghost peering inside the building. Puck put his arm over her shoulders and leaned his head on hers.

"I'm glad you're here," he said. "Greet can really use your support. Change is never easy. Even when it's for the best."

"What about Nel?" she asked. "She's eight years old and needs a full-time dad."

"I love her with all my heart." He sat straight and took her hand. "Kids are flexible at this age. She'll be fine with whatever Greet decides to do."

"I just can't believe this is happening," Annie held his hand in both of hers. "The two of you have been together almost as long as I can remember."

"Life happens, doesn't it? Just like it changed for you and Menno. The four of us were inseparable. Remember when we used to talk about buying a house and living together forever? It's a shame that things have to end. Maybe nothing really lasts." He inhaled then let out a slow breath. "Have you been down to the lighthouse yet?"

"I think I'd find too many painful memories there."

"No, Annie, you're wrong about that. The things from our child-hood are all good. I know your mom dying was tragic, but I'm talking about the other stuff. Being a kid on Bonaire. The ocean in our back-yard and the freedom to run loose with the best friends a person could ask for. Funny, all four of us fell in love with our besties. You and Menno, me and—" he cleared his throat, "Greet. People search for that all their lives and never find it."

"Puck, I have to ask." She wondered if he'd stop her. When he didn't, she continued, "What's going on? Why the split?"

"Sometimes people just want more than a marriage can provide."

"Puck!" A stranger yelled in the door. "She's gone. Come on and give us a hand. I've got a ten-foot tree with yours and Menno's names on it."

"Time for us to get to work." Puck stood and Annie did the same.

"Okay, but let's agree this conversation is far from over."

The church hall looked like Santa's workshop had exploded in it. Tables were covered with red and green decorations. Groups worked together to assemble greenery and plywood cutouts of all things Christmas. Garlands were draped over half the windows and giant candy canes lined the walls. Something similar to snowflakes wafted over a group trying to adhere material to a snowman scene. Father O'Brian saw Annie and Puck walk in and hurried over to say hello.

"Puck, what a shame, you just missed your wife," The Father said. "I think Menno's waiting for you to help carry the tree inside."

"I'm on it. See you later Annie?"

"I'm not staying long, but I would like that."

"Annie," Father O'Brian said. "I'm so glad you found the time to join us. Traditionally, we only ask adults to help, we want the little ones to have a nice surprise when they get here. It's a labor of love turning our everyday community room into a winter wonderland. But the looks on the kid's faces when they walk in is well worth the effort."

"I'd be happy to help with the tree." She hoped he didn't see beyond her enthusiasm.

"Let the men handle the sap and unruly branches. Why don't you give Orion a hand getting our Mr. and Mrs. Claus put together?"

"I'd be glad too." She felt excited to be able to spend time with Orion without being a blubbering mess.

"Martino!" Father O'Brian called across the room. "Don't put Rudolph in the manger scene!" He hurried off to right the blasphemous wrong.

Annie searched the hall and spotted Orion just beyond the group wrapping and tagging gifts. They had a list, no doubt indicating naughty or nice, and checked off names as they went.

"Annie, thank God," Orion said, then blessed herself. "I've got to get these two presentable and Mrs. Claus won't stop complaining."

Studying her immediate surroundings, Annie realized the Mr. and Mrs. Clause Father O'Brian wanted her to help with weren't wooden figurines or soft sculptures as she expected. They were actual people in various stages of undress.

"Annie, child," Orion said, "Let me introduce you to the lieutenant governor. He'll be playing Santa." The man stood in stocking feet and was bare chested. He wore a pair of Santa pants, the waistband straining against his girth. He smiled and nodded at Annie.

"Very nice to meet you." Annie had to give it to him. He had a tummy that would jiggle like a bowl full of jelly. His head was bald except for the ill attempt at a combover. His threads of hair did nothing to hide the shine bouncing off his scalp.

"And this is—" Orion began.

"I'm Dimphy." The woman cut in. She must've been Orion's age, but unlike the manicurist, Dimphy was fighting the gray. Her hair was dyed a unique shade of burgundy and piled high on her head. She wore large hoops and full make up complete with an alluring smokey eye. What struck Annie most was her outfit. It might have come from *Forever Twenty-One*. A black mini, heels and a shining red bustier top. "I'm the proprietor of *Bottoms Up*. My shop is just down the road from Orion's little nail place. Bottoms up, discrete playthings for the explorer in you."

Annie's eyebrows shot to the sky. Well, that would explain the outfit. "So nice to meet you Dimphy. Father O'Brian asked me to help with your outfits."

"Well, all I need is a Santa hat," Dimphy said.

"Mrs. Claus will *not* have her bosom spilling out of her top on my watch," Orion said. "You'll scare the kids away dressed like that." She held up a traditional felt red and white Mrs. Claus costume. "Put this on. What you're wearing now is essentially under garments. You can't hand out gifts to the children wearing your underwear at a church function."

"Well, who died and left *you* boss? I don't see why Mrs. Claus needs to look like a frumpy old spinster."

"*Look* like a spinster, Dimphy, you *are* an old spinster. You can't put lipstick on a pig!"

"I'll wear the dress." The lieutenant governor chimed in. All three shot him a questioning look and he simply shrugged his shoulders.

Father O'Brian settled it. Mrs. Claus would wear the customary costume. Once that was decided, a bigger challenge arose. The bowl full of jelly simply didn't fit into the red coat. Annie used a seam ripper and opened the sides of the jacket while Orion cut and measured additional fabric. They sat with the celebrated costume laid between them and stitched the extensions into place.

"Orion, you handled that well," Annie said. "For a minute there I thought we were going to have a PG-17 Christmas." She worked the needle into and out of the fabric until it was closed.

"Dimphy and I've been best friends since childhood. We've been arguing all our lives. It's how we communicate. I did get pretty upset when she stole the lieutenant governor away from his wife."

"What?" Her eyebrows went north for the second time.

"Come to find his wife Twila was happy to be rid of him. But that's a story for another time." She tied off her thread and broke it between her teeth. "Fingers crossed the hat will fit over his big head."

"Oh my." Father O'Brian returned. "I'd have more luck herding cats."

"What's happened now?" Annie asked.

"Silvia's daughter surprised her with an early Christmas gift," he said.

"That's wonderful," Orion said.

"No, it's terrible." His brows furrowed. "She's taking her to Paris."

"That's great," Annie said. "France for the holiday sounds amazing."

"No, it doesn't."

"Father, what do you have against Paris?" Orion asked.

"Nothing at all, but Silvia's our soloist for the Christmas Eve service. What are we going to do without her rendition of *O Holy Night?*"

"I think Dimphy's got some pipes on her," Orion said.

"Not on your life," he mumbled, and walked away.

Chapter Seven

"Now you look like a proper Mr. and Mrs. Claus." Orion held her chin and examined the couple.

Dimphy stood in her felt red and white dress, grey wig in place. She wore a pair of Mary Jane's, wire rimmed spectacles on the bridge of her nose, and heavy tights. Orion had brushed bright red cheeks on her and was quite pleased with the final product. Dimphy's face was sour.

"Now Dimphy," Father O'Brian said. "You know God would frown on us if we allowed Mrs. Claus to be anything but modestly dressed."

With her next assignment, Annie wove between volunteers and piles of stacked folding chairs. Her destination, the towering evergreen. It was erect and the lights had been strung. Boxes overflowing with balled up newspaper were piled off to the side. An eight foot step ladder had been placed near the branches.

"Hi Menno," Annie said. "Father O'Brian sent me to help with the tree."

"Annie, great," he said. "Puck got reassigned to the kitchen, I could use a keen eye. I didn't see your name on the list of volunteers."

"Originally, I didn't think I'd have the time to help. It sounds funny, but I was on the beach today and after a swim and a quick nap, inspiration hit me. I want to be involved."

"How about if you climb up and I'll pass you the ornaments?"

"Martha Stewart I am not, but I do possess the skill of placing them equidistant from each other."

Menno held the ladder steady as Annie climbed to the top. He fished a glass ball out of the nest of paper, added a hook and passed it to her. They continued working quietly and the upper boughs of the tree slowly came to life.

"Menno, since we've got the time, I have a few questions I hope you might answer for me."

"And what might they be?" He handed her a cotton ball snowman.

"You know that Greet asked me to come here and help her through this separation with Puck. I'm glad to do it, to support my friend, but I can't stop wondering if there's something more going on here. And, since you—"

"And Puck are friends, you think maybe I know something that would help to explain this whole estrangement."

"Exactly."

"I was hoping you were here to spend some time with me."

"Oh, that too. I didn't mean—"

"It's alright, no need to explain. Puck and I have had some long conversations about this very thing."

"You have?" She brightened.

"No, Annie," he laughed. "We haven't. Guys don't talk about this stuff."

"That's crazy."

"Maybe. But I do know he still loves her. He may not say it out loud, but since he left, he's been quiet and seems really down. For a while I thought maybe she threw him out. That's the way he's been acting. But I know that Greet would never do that."

Annie sat on the top step and held an ornament in her hand. "So, he doesn't have a girlfriend on the side?"

"Are you kidding?" Menno smiled. "He's not interested in other women. He loves Greet."

"He sure has a funny way of showing it. The mystery between those two continues, and the longer it goes on, the more that family is going to hurt." She placed the bobble. "Have you put a tree up at your place?"

"Of course." He handed her a white sea urchin with a red bow on it. "It's on my front porch. I don't know why I do it. I always spend the holiday with my parents at their place. I guess I do it for the kids in the neighborhood."

"Your mom and dad are doing well?"

"Better than that. They're close to retirement. I hear travel plans being made. Thanks for asking about them. They'd love to see you."

"I'm afraid I'm not staying long. I need to get this marriage put back together before I catch my flight tomorrow." She watched as his face darkened. "Wish me luck."

"Tomorrow? You just got here yesterday."

"I'm afraid I've got work to get back to. I'm in charge of this huge merger—"

"I can't believe you finally show up and stay for a total of two days." His cheerful expression was gone. "That's not much time. What if you can't do it? Saving a marriage in only a couple of days, what if you fail?"

"Then I'll pass the torch to you."

"Please reconsider your travel plans. Stay longer, spend Christmas with me."

"I'm expected back home. Stewart and my Aunt Peggy are counting on me spending the holiday with them."

"So, I may not see you again." He said, handing her a candy cane made of beads. "After the holidays, when the merger is complete, come back. Promise me you'll do that."

"I may be able to sneak away before the wedding." She placed the red and white cane on a branch.

The choir gathered and practiced carols in the loft as the hall full of volunteers continued with their tasks. The recognizable hymns drifted down and sent chills up Annie's arms. The music was so familiar she wished she could swim in the warm voices forever. The scent of honey baked ham and roasting turkey had her looking toward the kitchen.

Menno began to hum *Silent Night* and Annie sang quietly with the choir. A team placed hurricane candles on rows of dinner tables. They would be lit later that evening. A woman stopped at the tree with a tray of hot apple cider. Menno thanked her and took two cups.

Annie turned and sat on one of the ladder's steps. Cradling the warm mug, she blew on it and took a sip. The conductor brought the choir to an end then yelled down from the loft.

"Hey everyone!" he called. "Raise your voices and sing along to this next song."

After hearing the first three notes of *Angels We Have Heard on High*, the entire room broke into song. Annie laughed as Menno mimed being out of air while holding the long notes at the chorus.

When the song ended and her cup was empty, Annie climbed down and Menno moved the stepladder around to the next set of branches. Up she went again.

"Here's a unique one." He held a wreath made out of elbow pasta. Clumps of glue covered most of it and a thin green ribbon had been attached for hanging. "Someone had a good time making this. I've hung it on this tree over the past three years."

"I love it." Annie reached out but just as her fingers touched his, her phone buzzed. Without a thought, she pulled her hand away to search for her cell. The child's Christmas contribution crashed to the floor. Annie mouthed, *I'm sorry,* and touched her screen.

"Richard, hello." She climbed down and stood next to the half decorated tree. "No, this is a fine time, I'm not busy at all. What's up?" She held the phone to her ear and her other hand on her hip. While listening to her boss she watched Menno as he found a broom and began sweeping up the broken mess. The organ joined the choir who sang with growing enthusiasm. Annoyed with the inability to hear her boss, she cupped her free hand to her ear and walked out of the hall.

Annie cleared a spot in the snow and sat on the church steps. She conversed with her boss while brushing accumulating flakes off her shoulders. She knew this proposal like a mother knows her own child. She explained the numbers and he asked questions until they both understood the specific terms the clients had concerns with. She touched End and stood to stretch. Tina's Gelato Shop was two blocks away and she definitely had earned a treat.

"Hi Valentina," Annie said. The owner gave her a pleasant smile but Annie was sure she didn't remember her. "May I have a scoop of peppermint stick?" She grew uncomfortable as the shop owner seemed to study her. Then Valentina opened the cooler and found a scoop.

"Would you like that on a cone or in a dish?" Valentina appeared to look beyond her stiff outfit and heels. She seemed to ignore the fine Italian leather wallet Annie was searching through.

"Cone, please."

Valentina looked into her eyes, obviously studying the familiar curve of her cheeks, and turn of her smile. "Annie Martis." She dropped the scoop. "Come here girl." She circled from behind the ice cream cooler and met Annie with a hug. "You're finally home again. We all knew you'd come back."

"I didn't think you remembered me." Annie was surprised to feel a tear forming.

"It took me just a minute. I'd never forget Rose's girl. Welcome home."

After catching up with her mother's friend, Annie sat on the bench in front of the shop. She caught drips with her tongue before they could fall. A familiar figure walked down the sidewalk across from her. The fisherman she'd watched unloading his catch earlier that day was heading home. He looked at the ground and walked with his shoulders slumped over. Annie wondered if he had adapted this posture in order to hide the scar that disfigured his face. Her cell buzzed.

"Richard." A feeling this call wouldn't be short, she stood and dropped her cone into the trash bin. "What's up?"

She jogged back to Greet's house and opened her laptop. Nel and her mother were in the kitchen. They would have to leave for the church soon. Annie brought up the documents she needed and returned Richard's call.

"Okay, I'm here. I've got the final numbers in front of me."

Thirty minutes later, Annie didn't hear Nel come down the stairs. She never knew the young girl had tried to get her attention and asked her to hang up the phone. An hour had passed when the call finally ended. The sun was beginning to set when she took the time to look again, double checking that all the figures were correct.

Certain the client team was misunderstanding the information, Annie rued her decision to leave New York at such a crucial time. Stretching her arms over her head, she walked around the empty home. She had a vague recollection of motioning to Greet to go ahead without her. Did she notice them carrying the castle out the door? If so, it was only a blur.

She checked the time. If she left right now she might still make the competition. She used the bathroom and redid her hair. Her stomach rumbled. If she hurried, she might get a plate of that ham and turkey that had smelled so intoxicating. Having left the tree half decorated, she looked forward to seeing it in all its lighted glory.

After pulling the door shut, she headed down the street. But her thoughts were tangled in the conversation with her boss. Did she explain to him that the data she'd proposed was only reliable until the end of the quarter? Maybe that was where all the confusion laid. And did the client understand the values were fluid and fully dependent on the S&P 500? So many working parts and the entire deal relied on all of them coming together perfectly. Stopping in her tracks, she watched the snow fly just two blocks away. Planning to be back in New York tomorrow, she would head into the office straight from the airport. She took a step and stopped again. But what if that was too late? The client team seemed to be charging toward a new deadline. Were they purposefully storming ahead, trying to close the deal by the end of the year? She could see families tromping through the snow, clearly headed to San Bernardo. She turned around and walked back to the house.

Annie was sound asleep on the sofa. Cell phone in her hand and laptop on the coffee table when Nel and Greet walked in. She woke with the sound of the door closing and sat up. Disoriented, she checked the time and looked around the room. Nel carried her castle with a big blue ribbon hanging from a turret. But instead of being overjoyed that she had won, tracks of dried tears marked her red cheeks. She ignored her aunt and without stopping, took the first-prize winner upstairs to her room.

"She won?" Annie's voice was scratchy with sleep.

"She did." Greet hung her coat and switched off the porch light. "Goodnight, Annie."

"Wait Greet. What's wrong? Did something happen?" Annie pictured Puck making a scene. "Puck didn't do anything stupid, did he?"

Greet stopped with one foot on the stair. "You really think this is about Puck? For as smart as you are, you're actually pretty dumb." She stopped herself and took a breath. "You didn't show up for her. For Nel. You two were a team and you didn't even come down to the church."

"But I had to—"

"She'd been looking forward to showing you off to her friends, who were all there with their families. All night, she kept looking toward the door. Looking for you, Annie."

"I'm sorry, I was there this afternoon. I helped—"

"Menno told me. You volunteered for as long as the time was convenient for you. As soon as the boss called, you left him flat. The same way you just left Nel." She put her palm on her forehead then drug it over her head. "Ignore my text messages and my phone calls. Walk out on Menno, I don't care about any of that. But when you hurt my little girl, you've crossed the line. I love you Annie, but maybe you just don't fit in here anymore."

The fresh air and all the activity left Annie sleeping like a log. She gradually woke to sounds of Greet and Nel downstairs in the kitchen. The sun gradually lightened her room in the early morning hours. Pulling the disheveled blankets up around her shoulders, she thought about the correspondence she had with Richard the day before. Surely everything was settled now.

As she stretched her arms overhead and pushed her toes downward, she remembered Nel's teary face when she returned from church the night before. Greet's strong words had left an impression. If the little girl was still upset, Annie would be sure to tell her how sorry she was for missing the event.

The unmistakable scent of freshly brewed coffee snuck into her room. She pushed off the comforter and hopped out of bed. Laying her luggage on the mattress, she folded her items from the closet and placed them inside. She emptied the drawer and tucked her underthings around the sides.

"Good morning." Annie stopped at the kitchen door. Nel feigned interest in her cereal and didn't bother to look up. Greet poured two mugs and placed them both on the table.

"How did you sleep?" Greet's voice was raspy.

"Very well, thanks." Annie pulled out her chair and tried to gauge the cold welcome. "May I join you?"

"Don't be silly," Greet said. "You're a guest in this house. Please, have a seat." She nudged her daughter. "Are you going to say good morning?"

Nel's eyes shot to her aunt and then darted back to her cereal. "Morning," she mumbled.

Annie added cream to her cup, her spoon tinged as she stirred. Greet rested her elbows on the table, held her coffee in both hands but never took a sip. Nel's spoon scraped around her bowl but she didn't eat, the flakes had grown soggy. The air was heavy and the kitchen silent.

What's happening here? Annie wondered. She missed the community dinner at the church last night and these two seemed deeply wounded. Was attending the gingerbread house contest really that important? She knew what was really important, closing this business deal. They obviously don't understand the time, effort, and commitment multimillion dollar contracts require. Not to mention her twenty-four-seven schedule, unspoken, but agreed to. It's what it takes to be successful on Wall Street.

Annie sipped her coffee and studied the gloomy faces sitting with her. They clearly didn't understand. But she must admit, although her own goals were clear, she was having trouble appreciating what was important to them.

Nel's expression this morning spoke one thousand words. The child had been hurt. Annie promised to help her with the castle and agreed they were a team. Nel was looking forward to introducing her aunt to Snowball Charlie and she was a no show. With Nel's usually cheerful disposition gone, something inside Annie pulled her heart down. Clearly it was her actions that did this to the sweet girl.

She glanced at Greet's own downward turned face. Her complexion still dull and her eyelids looking heavy. She had invited

Annie here for the express purpose of helping her through this breakup. Annie had done nothing of the sort and now had caused unrest between the three of them. It was hard to admit, but she realized she was being a complete ass.

"I owe you both an apology," Annie said. "I won't deluge you with excuses but I will ask you to forgive me. I'm sorry. I should've been at the church last night, it was important to you. Nel and I were a team and I let my best mate down." After no response she continued. "In all fairness my schedule was cleared before I came to Bonaire. This thing that's taking up all my time was a done deal already. We weren't planning to work again until after the first of the year but the client has questions." Still, no reaction from either of them. She sipped her coffee then put the mug down.

"Whatever." Nel whispered.

Annie studied her niece's face. The heartbreak there was painful to see. Uncle Joe's warnings over the years now sounded clear. "My uncle told me this would happen," she said. "He said I was letting my job take over my life. But he was wrong." She swallowed as the reality sank in. "I don't have any life to take. I've gladly given it all over to Global World Bank. My job is my life, it's a choice I made. Greet, I still consider you my best friend, but you're the best of one. You're my only friend. Uncle Joe has been trying to warn me. He sees my lack of a social life and the total absence of fun. He knows that bank will be the end of me, and yet I'm still beholden to it."

Nel looked at her, some of the hardness softening. "You should tell your uncle he was wrong. You have friends. Mom and me."

"Thanks, Nel. But the jokes on me," Annie touched her eye. "I've missed out on so much. Greet, you have so many lifelong friends, they could've been mine, too".

Greet took Annie's hand. "They are yours. Menno, Corrie, Puck, we've all been waiting for you to come home. We never stopped being here for you."

"We can be your friends and family," Nel said.

"There's nothing I'd like more." The atmosphere lifted.

Greet stood behind Annie and gave her a hug. "It's not all gloom and doom. You've made a full life in New York. We just live a different one here. And I'm sorry about what I said last night. I was upset. You fit in just fine."

Nel's chair squeaked and she threw her arms around her aunt. "We have more fun here."

"I'm not going to argue with that," Annie said as they released her. "How about a fresh start? I'm going to cancel today's flight and extend my stay. Let me treat you to a girls' day. How about if I start by making us pancakes?" She hopped up and searched the refrigerator. "With whipped cream." She held a red and white can and shook it up and down. "I'm completely aware this is a bribe, but maybe an overdose of sugar will make us all happy again."

"Can we add blueberries?" Nel started to brighten.

"Nel, we used those in the muffins we made," Greet said.

Annie searched and held up a bag of chocolate chips. "Even better. Greet, you're off from the salon today and Nel's done with school until after the new year. Later this morning let's stop in the square and I can teach you how to make a proper snowman. Hot chocolate at the bakery?" Nel nodded. "And I need some Christmas gift ideas for a little girl I know."

"Me?" She bounced in her seat when Annie nodded.

"I'm supposed to talk to Stewart after breakfast to confirm my arrival time," Annie said. "I'll let him know I'm staying a bit longer and there's no need to pick me up at the airport today. We can get started as soon as I finish my call with him."

"Is Stewart your prince?" Nel brightened.

"Not exactly royalty but he *is* my fiancé." She checked the time. "We have a call at nine-thirty. We're going to talk for fifteen minutes. Then I'm all yours."

"Wait." Greet said. "What? You reserved a time for a phone call with the man you love?"

"Yes. Of course. He's at work and on a schedule."

"And you already know how long you're going to talk?"

"Yes, that's the time we both allotted. Why that look on your face?"

"That explains a lot. Annie, we love you. But girl, you have got to lighten up."

Chapter Eight

"Great to talk to you too." Annie sat on the sofa listening to Stewart on the other end. Nel was assembling a Lego figure on the floor. "I'll send you the new flight information. Okay, bye." She touched End.

"Was that your fiancé?"

"Yes, it was."

"You forgot to say I love you."

"I didn't forget." Oddly, she felt the need to explain. "It's implied."

"You don't have to say it because it's in pie?" Nel squinted.

"Yes, that's right." Annie tried to remember the last time she and Stewart had told each other they loved one another. But she couldn't even recall the first time they had use those words. She looked at her blank screen and turned her cell in her hands. Was it possible they never declared their love for one another? No worry, as she had just explained, it was implied.

Nel insisted on wearing her pink fairy outfit and carrying her magic wand. The dress was almost as big as she was. It had a sash with the word *Princess* written in glitter. They sat at a table on the patio of one of Greet's favorite eateries. Surrounded by a flowery motif and sipping Aperol spritz, the restaurant inadvertently catered to women. The tables overlooked the water, today there wasn't a cloud in the sky. Two ladies in tennis skirts, sitting at the table next to theirs, shared a chef salad. Nearer the water, a group of four played bridge.

"This place is wonderful," Annie said.

A warm breeze trickled onshore as she looked out at the ocean. Colorful sailboats flew by on the turquoise water. The establishment had created a fifteen foot seawall to keep the ocean at bay. Children played in the sand on the raised bed and entertained themselves while their moms finished lunch.

One small boy had gathered stones and was tossing them over the edge. He watched as they splashed into the water below. His mother called to him to move away from the steep fall. The child stamped his feet, threw the remaining stones to the ground, and thumped down on his diapered bottom. The young one's mother came and scooped him up before the tantrum could progress.

Annie enjoyed a blackened salmon salad. It had just the right amount of spice. Greet only picked at her lobster ravioli. She had hardly eaten a thing since Annie arrived. Nel gobbled up a child sized serving of macaroni and cheese then ran off to play. After the server had cleared their plates, they ordered specialty coffees over ice. Both feeling pleasantly relaxed, they watched Nel as she occupied herself with the other children in the play area.

"Your daughter has me thinking." Annie watched Nel gather her frilly skirt and plop down in the sand.

"Oh? About what?" Greet sipped from the red straw in her glass.

"Stewart and I never say I love you. It's implied of course, but we never actually say those words. I don't know if we ever have."

"That's—" She stopped herself from saying *terrible*. "Why do you think that is? Do you love him?"

"Sure. We're perfect together. He's working as a top advisor, for whom we think, will be the next governor of New York. If the campaign goes as we expect, the candidate should be offering Stewart a department head position in her cabinet. All I have to do is hold steady at Global World." Looking at her beautiful surroundings she thought of her office building. The cramped ride up in the elevator, the business grade wall to wall, and the cold glass windows that overlooked other buildings.

"If that's really what you want. You said yourself—"

"It's not only about what *I* want. Stewart's hoping to hold a public office by the time I'm jabbing at manager. It's important for him to have a successful wife."

"What does any of this have to do with being in love?"

"But we are. Maybe not like you and Puck, more like—"

"A merger? Like Time and Warner, Smith and Wesson? This all sounds more like a business deal than a marriage."

"I don't know Greet. Are there different kinds of love?"

"I'm not sure. But Annie, don't you want to find out?"

A scream came from the ladies playing bridge. "Someone help her! She fell in!"

Annie sprung to her feet. The tablecloth came with her as she took off at a run. She scanned the play area for Nel but didn't see her anywhere. People were lined on the seawall looking down into the water.

"Nel!" Greet yelled, her panic growing. "Where's Nel?"

Annie flung herself over the wall and plunged fifteen feet into the water below. As she surfaced for a breath, a wave crashed into her and drove her against the solid structure. Inhaling a second time, she was again rammed against the barrier. Once the water retreated, she dove below the surface. A cloud of pink tulle was sinking underneath her. Nel's legs were trapped within the once flowing fabric and her sparkly sash confined her arms. In her hand she clutched the magic fairy wand.

With her target in sight, Annie dug with her arms and kicked her legs as the young girl sank farther away from her. She swam deeper. Her arm muscles began to scream and her tired legs wobbled. Her lungs were begging for air when she caught up to the child. She wrapped her in a tight embrace, planted her feet on the sand and propelled them both skyward.

They broke the surface like a rocket. Annie sucked in full breaths of air and floated on her back. She cradled unresponsive Nel in front of her.

"Call for help!" She yelled to the crowd gathered above her and searched for a way out. The seawall ran several hundred yards in both directions. They were trapped where they floated. "Nel? Nel, can you hear me?" With no sign of life, Annie turned her head and gave a quick and forceful breath into the girl's mouth. "Nel?" She did it a second time and Nel responded with several forceful coughs. Spray flew from her mouth as she choked out the ocean water.

"Thank God." Annie's heart slowed.

"Aunt Annie?"

"I'm here. Rest back on me. I'll keep you afloat." Annie allowed herself to relax. "Are you doing okay there?"

"I fell in."

"You sure did. We're going to wait right here until they come and get us." She could see all the commotion above them. Confident that help was on the way, she closed her eyes and only thought of the sun shining on her face. They rose and fell with the swell. Annie held her palm on the girl's rib cage and could feel it moving air in and out.

"Nel?" Annie gave her a little shake but got no response. "You rest little one. I've got you."

Only minutes had passed when Annie heard the heavy hum of a motorboat approaching. *Bonaire Water Rescue* was printed across the hull. The engine eased up as it came near and the four person crew tossed two life preservers in to aid them.

Annie untangled the sash from around Nel and slipped the ring over her head and around her sluggish body. Nel draped her arms across the brightly colored device then her head fell to the side.

"Are either of you hurt?" Menno asked from the boat.

"She wasn't breathing when I got her to the surface," Annie said.

"I gave her two rescue breaths and she worked a lot of water out of her lungs. She was talking to me but now seems exhausted."

Menno and his coworker entered the water with a spine board. "We'll be extra cautious and use this just in case." They expertly maneuvered the board and had the young girl attached to it and up on the boat in no time.

Annie swam toward the ladder at the stern. She grabbed ahold of the rails but her foot slipped off the first rung. She realized she still had her heels on. Pulling off one shoe then the other, she tossed them onto the deck. Once on board she steadied herself as she watched the bright day go dim. She swayed and searched for something to hang on to.

"Whoa there," Menno held her waist. "Looks like you didn't come out of this totally unscathed." He touched her head and looked at the blood on his finger.

"I was pushed into the seawall when I first jumped in." She held her hand to her scalp. "I didn't realize it got me."

"Aunt Annie, are you okay? You're bleeding." Nel laid strapped to the board. Tears ran from her eyes.

"I'm fine." But as she spoke, Nel went out of focus. "No need to worry about—"

Menno caught her as she slumped to the deck.

———

"There you are." Menno stood next to Annie's cot and watched her as she regained consciousness. "You're safe in the emergency room. Everything is going to be okay." A silly old Christmas hit song played over the speakers hidden in the tile ceiling.

"Is Nel all right?" She pulled herself into a sitting position and held her head.

"She's going to be fine. They told Greet to take her home and let her get some rest."

"How long have I been here?" She was wearing a hospital gown and her hair was partially dry.

"About an hour. We're waiting for the doctor to read the CT scan they took. She wants to rule out any skull fractures or internal bleeding."

"They took a scan? I don't remember it. They may find my head full of cobwebs. Everything seems a little fuzzy." The irritating song came to its chorus. "I feel like I'm the one who got ran over by the reindeer and Grandma's at home doing fine."

"You've got six stitches on the side of your head."

Annie tenderly touched her hair and found what felt like tiny pins sticking out of her scalp.

"They used the dissolvable kind so you don't have to come back to get anything removed." He put his hand on her shoulder. "Nice job today. I heard the heroic story of you catapulting yourself into the great abyss and pulling Nel to the surface. You saved her life."

"Anyone could've done it." She squinted in the bright light of the hospital.

"Don't sell yourself short. Of all the people at that restaurant today, you were the only one who jumped in."

"Annie Martis?" A woman wearing a white lab coat and holding a tablet approached them.

"Yes, that's me."

"I'm Dr. Stevenson." She scanned the test results on her screen. "I've been assigned to your case. May I?" She pulled a small light from her pocket and flashed it in each of Annie's eyes. "Follow me." Holding up an index finger, she moved it side to side. "You appear fine and the scan checks out okay. Looks like you suffered a spell of syncope. It's no wonder with all that was going on."

"I fainted?"

"Yes, but the fact that you did hit your head gives me cause to take some precautions." The doctor held her wrist and checked her pulse. "How do you feel?"

"I've got a bit of a headache. Other than that, I feel okay."

"I'll give you a prescription strength anti-inflammatory, they should calm that head. I'm going to clear you to leave the hospital but with restrictions. No driving for twenty four hours and no vigorous activity. If you experience any dizziness or if that headache gets worse, come back in to see me."

"Thank you, doctor."

"Miss Martis," the doctor said. "You did a wonderful thing saving that young girl today. You're the talk of the town."

"Nel's my niece. I'd do anything for her." As she said the words, she was struck at how true they were. Having broken the child's heart earlier, the empathy and compassion she felt for her were now strong. She had disappointed the young girl once and promised herself never to do that again.

A nurse brought paperwork for Annie to sign and a child-proof pill bottle with her name on it. A copy of the instructions she was to follow were given to her along with a bag of her clothes and shoes. Menno helped her off the cot and stood ready to assist if she experienced any dizziness. Annie removed her dress from the bundle and held the soaking wet fabric in front of her.

"What time is your flight? I'd be happy to drive you to the airport."

"I cancelled it. I had to straighten some things out before I left. Please don't ask."

"So, you're staying? That's great. I can bring you some dry clothes. Will you spend the afternoon with me?"

"Is that a bribe?" She examined her drenched leather shoes and then stuffed it all back in the bag.

"Honestly, I'll feel better if I can keep an eye on you."

"Thank you, that's very kind. I'm sure Greet has enough to worry about looking after Nel. It's just as well I leave them alone. I bet she could use some quiet after all that's happened. I appreciate your offer."

"Wait here. I've got a few things in my locker at the firehouse. I'll run down there and be right back."

Twenty minutes later he returned and handed Annie some items. She pulled the curtain around the cot and removed the gown. She stepped into a pair of gym shorts. Thankfully, Menno's waist was thin and the elastic band fit. Her curves helped keep things in place. She pulled a light cotton sweatshirt over her head. The hem fell to her thighs and the sleeves swallowed her arms and hands. She checked her hair and found her bun half way down her back. She pulled at the elastic and let the locks fall free.

"I'm afraid I don't have any shoes in your size." Menno said from the other side of the drape. "Ironically, back when I knew you, they were always optional."

Annie pulled the screen along the rail. "What do you think?" She stood in the too big outfit and wiggled her toes.

"I think I can help you out a bit." She followed him to the nurses' station. A man there handed him a pair of scissors and Menno proceeded to cut off both sleeves. "Now you look like you could workout with the firefighters."

———

"I called Greet," Menno said. "Nel's asleep and Greet sounds dog-tired. She asked about you. I told her the doctor gave you the okay and you're spending some time with me." He opened the passenger side door and Annie climbed in the pickup truck. "With any luck Nel won't have a clear memory of what happened." He closed the door and circled the front of the vehicle.

As Menno climbed in behind the wheel, Annie studied the view out the window. "Now that you have me where are we off to?"

"If it's not too bold I'd like to take you to my place. I know your head is hurting. I thought we could sit on the porch and watch the waves roll in. That might be as much excitement as you can handle right now."

"That sounds really nice. I think those pills Dr. Stevenson gave me are starting to ease the headache. The light isn't causing nearly as much sensitivity." He started the engine and she fastened her seatbelt. She noticed the *Bonaire Fire Department* logo printed on her too large sweatshirt. "Are you a fireman?"

"EMT. Emergency medical technician. It's a volunteer position that works closely with the fire department. When the call came in that a child had fallen over the seawall, I was alerted and met up with the rescue squad."

"It was all a bit surreal. There I was, floating with Nel, waiting to be pulled out of the water. When I looked up and saw you, I wasn't surprised at all. I thought, of course Menno is here, he's going to save us."

"Menno to the rescue. I should have a bumper sticker made."

"I've always been able to count on you. You were the anchor that kept me from floating away when times got tough. Today, you showed up for me again. Thank you, Menno."

"All in a day's work, no need to thank me."

"I'm sorry for ditching you at the church hall."

"I was quite capable of getting that tree decorated by myself."

"I know that, but leaving was a loser move on my part. I see that now."

"It wasn't as much fun," he said. "When you left, the whole holiday spirit went with you. No one to laugh and sing with."

"For what it's worth, I was having a good time too."

As they drove through town Annie kept pointing out businesses she remembered as a teen. She would ask him about a particular store or building and he gave her the update.

"Mr. Crowley retired and moved to Aruba," he said. "He sold the grocery to a local named Graaf. Do you remember Deek Graaf from our class?" Annie nodded. "His dad bought the store and Deek works with him." They made a turn and he pointed out another new establishment. "They built the hotel four years ago. Very bougie, I'm told. It has a five star restaurant off the lobby." A large Christmas tree sat near the entrance and evergreen wreaths hung on the double doors.

"Five stars? Really?"

"Who knows, I mean, who exactly gives out the stars?" They laughed. "How do we know it's not on a scale of ten?"

"Right. Five out of ten, the place could be a total dive."

They drove along a road parallel to the ocean and she watched a flamboyance of flamingos wading in the surf.

"The more I see of it, the more I realize the island really has changed," she said. "I guess I imagined everything would wait for me, frozen in time. You, Greet and Corrie. I half expected that you'd be just like I left you. I'd come to Bonaire and just slide in between everyone, pick up where we all left off." She whispered, "It's what I wished it would be like."

A cheerfully annoying Christmas song came on the radio and Menno clicked it off. He downshifted as they drove over the narrower streets.

As they passed through town some long forgotten sites triggered memories of growing up on the island. Her home was always filled with people who sat on that grey line between friend and family. As her life in New York expanded, she stopped thinking quite as much about the community that existed on Bonaire. Sure, she and her aunt had met the family that lived in the brownstone next door, but she would be hard pressed to describe them as friends.

Everywhere on the island she looked she saw her mother. She chose to remember her as a vibrant woman and still full of life. As a college graduate, her mom came to Bonaire to volunteer for the dolphin tracking program. She loved the ocean and sea life and worked during her free time to educate others on how to conserve it. Sometime during her summer here, she met and fell in love with an island boy, Annie's dad.

When Annie's father walked down the streets in town, people moved to the side and gave him his space. She recalled her hand being lost in his baseball mitt sized grip. He was a fisherman by trade and was often covered in saltwater and fish guts. The physical demands of the job resulted in broad shoulders and tree trunk legs. Annie was so proud of her father she stood straighter as they wandered along the streets of Kralendijk hand in hand.

Her mother was fair and stood just five feet tall. Her petiteness was in strong contrast to her booming personality and get-it-done attitude. Annie remembered when a local family lost everything to a fire that had ripped through their modest home. Sometime during the night, worn electrical cords came into contact with the home's insulation. The family of four were lucky to have escaped with their lives.

The following day Annie was sharing her bedroom with their two children. The parents slept on the sofa her mother had made up in the downstairs room. That entire week her mom strapped on her jetpack and blew through town assembling a team that would help get this family back on track. The task could have proved daunting, but this was not just any family on any remote island. Although saddened to have lost their lot in life, they were surrounded by a community that wouldn't let them suffer. They belonged to Bonaire.

"You're a million miles away," Menno said.

"Not miles exactly, years. I was just thinking about the night the Sevilla's house burned down. This town rallied like they'd been practicing all their lives for that catastrophe. The family never needed a shelter or aid from the government. Everyone came together to help them."

"Their two daughters are both in high school now. They still live in the house the town rebuilt."

He slowed the truck and turned onto a street leading to the beach. After half a block he took a left and drove onto an unpaved road. The houses were all one story and had stucco exteriors. They were each brightly painted in different colors. Menno pulled into the drive of the third house on the right. The façade was a pretty seafoam green and the window trims and storm shutters a bright white.

"Welcome to my place," he said. "Stay there, I'll get your door."

The houses on this side of the road were elevated enough to give a clear sightline over the homes across from them. It provided a perfect view of the ocean as it lapped at the beach nearby. Menno helped Annie out of the truck and they climbed the five steps to his covered front porch.

To the right was a full sized Christmas tree. It was strung with lights but other than those, had no additional decorations. At the top was what appeared to be a hand crocheted angel. Her wings were made of gossamer fabric and her hallo a ring of tiny seashells.

To the left a charcoal grill was tucked away in the corner. Ashen fingerprints dotted the black domed hood and a long spatula hung from the handle. Two comfortable chairs sat on the weathered wooden deck each with a sturdy cushion attached. Near the front door Menno had kicked off a pair of hiking boots with mud dried on the soles. A low table ran in front of the seats and a few items there caught Annie's attention.

"Will you be comfortable sitting out here?" he asked. "Maybe the fresh air will help clear your head."

"Yes, this is perfect, and the view is amazing."

"I'll fix something warm to drink and find us a little snack. Please, make yourself at home." Annie sat and as he opened the door to go inside, a golden retriever trotted out. "Stay here Ginger, no running off."

The dog put her chin in Annie's lap. Without thinking, she stroked the soft head then peeked inside the front window. When she was sure he was busy in the kitchen, she picked up a wicker basket from the table and dug through the contents.

"Let's see, three balls of yarn and a pair of knitting needles." The skeins were all tangled together. She lifted the work and thought it might one day be a winter scarf. She studied the woolen piece in progress and changed her mind. It was more a lopsided square, or was it? "Ginger, is your mom knitting a sweater?"

Hearing her name, the dog tilted her head.

She returned the bundle to its spot and glanced over her shoulder confirming the coast was still clear. A book had caught her eye. A receipt from the grocery store worked as a bookmark and she opened it to that page. She read the chapter title, "I married the count." Closing the pages, she then tilted her own head at the corset strung maiden on the cover. "Your mom likes romance novels." She replaced the paperback exactly where she had found it. "Knitting, romance novels and handmade angels. Ginger," she fell back in the chair, "Menno has neglected to tell me he's married."

Stupid her. Why did she think it was a good idea to completely disconnect from her friends on Bonaire? She had missed so much. Her bestie's marriage fell apart right under her nose. Annie never saw it coming and when Greet had explained it all to her over the phone, she was unprepared to say anything to help. Perhaps she couldn't have saved the marriage, but she absolutely could've been a better friend. And Nel. Sweet Nel had been so eager to have a relationship with Annie. She was excited to finally meet her unknown aunt. What a shame to have missed her first eight years of life.

But the biggest in-your-face fact was that the man she once loved was now married. How could she not have seen it? Greet had held fast to Annie's request to limit all discussion of Menno. Hearing about him those years ago only made it more difficult to let him go. Conversations carefully steered clear of his name and eventually Annie's own curiosity faded. At least that's what she told herself.

"How's your head?" Menno joined her on the porch and offered her a hot tea. "I thought this might help. Peppermint. The menthol is supposed to sooth migraines."

"Thank you for this. My head is feeling much better."

He put a wooden cutting board with slices of lemon Biscotti in front of her. She cradled the warm mug in her palms.

"I'm surprised you're still on the island. I know your flight home was today. Why the delay?"

"I made a disaster of something and needed to set it right. I have a flight out tomorrow."

"No matter the reason, I'm glad you're still here."

"This tea smells wonderful." She blew on the surface and remembered her borrowed outfit. "I'll be sure Greet gets these clothes back to you. I'll leave them at her place." She inadvertently touched her head and found her long locks tumbling over her shoulders. "I must look like a complete mess."

"Not at all." He sat in the adjacent chair. "On the contrary. You finally look like yourself. I was beginning to wonder if your hair would be permanently stuck in that tight ball."

"It's important for me to look professional." She reached for a cookie and dipped it in her tea. "My job requires it."

"You're not at work Annie, you're home. Relax and go barefoot. When was the last time you did that?"

"Relax?" She smiled. "What exactly does that mean? It's not in my vocabulary." She crossed her legs and wiggled her toes. She dipped the Biscotti in her mug. "I didn't have any shoes on the last time I took a shower, so there."

"God, I missed you. I still can't believe you're sitting here. All these years I thought I'd never see you again. I'm a little upset with Greet. She never mentioned you were coming home. If you and Nel hadn't needed those supplies, I may not have seen you."

"Don't be mad at Greet." She bit into the soft cookie. "I think I have her trained too well."

"What do you mean?"

"When I left Bonaire, of course you know I was crushed. Can you imagine being taken away from everything you know and love? New York was a shock to me. The noise, the smells, the constant thrum of energy. Life runs at a different pace there. It took me years to get used to it."

"I was happy to keep in touch," he said. "Calls and text messages. I was all in."

"But it was doing neither of us any good. I stayed down and depressed. Our conversations were filled with *I miss you* and *nothings the same without you*. Each time after we hung up, I'd feel lower than dirt."

"Me too," Menno said. "I just wish you'd had some faith in me."

"I had no idea you were thinking of transferring to Columbia University. I'd cut all ties and I'm so sorry about that. It's no excuse, but seventeen year old me made choices I never would make now."

They quietly watched as boats sped over the water, returning guests to their resorts. Thoughts of *what if* like a whisper in a long ago dream teased Annie's thoughts. A large commercial fishing vessel headed out to sea for the evening's catch. Fishermen's voices drifted over the water and touched them on the porch.

Annie finished her cookie and took a second. Two women were talking as they walked down the road. They waved at Menno and Annie then climbed the porch steps to join them.

"Hi Orion, Dimphy," Menno said. He stood and offered his seat but neither took it.

"Is that Annie Martis?" Orion asked.

"Yes, Orion, it's me." She giggled.

"Well, you look a little more like yourself," Orion said. "Good for you child. Menno, be sure to talk sweet to her. She doesn't get enough of that up north."

"She saved a little girl's life today," Dimphy said. She wore her signature outfit, clearly chosen off the racks of her naughty lingerie shop. "It's all anybody will talk about." She studied Annie. "Lord knows why you're wearing that horrible outfit. You'll never catch a man in that. Even Menno, who's been pining for you all these years, won't ask you out if you insist on wearing oversized workout clothes."

Annie felt the heat rise up her neck and saw Menno's face flush. Was Dimphy's comment true?

"Dimphy," Orion said. "For crying out loud. Is that anyway to talk to our lost sheep? Besides, she's engaged."

"Oh, Orion get a clue, we're women. We're always in the market, isn't that right, Annie?"

"No, actually, I'm getting marri—"

"You know what I'm going to do for this town's new hero?"

Dimphy asked. "I'm going to give you twenty percent off any nightie or bustier in my shop."

Annie's eyes went wide and her mouth momentarily hung open. "Thank you." She caught herself and smiled. "That's so nice."

"Stop by in the morning. I have a black leather number that will do wonders for you."

———

"How are you feeling?" Menno asked, once their visitors had left. "Up for an early dinner in town?"

Annie wanted to say yes, more time with Menno was just what she wanted. Sadly, from what she could see, he was in a relationship with someone. She felt disappointed in him for so easily forgetting that. Then she reminded herself she was engaged to be married. What was she doing here?

"Maybe we should call it a day." She forced the words out. "Won't your wife be home soon?"

"I have a wife?"

"Girlfriend, then. I'm sure she wouldn't want to run into an old flame of yours sitting on her porch."

"No girlfriend at the time," he said. "Unless you know something I don't."

"I know that basket is filled with knitting materials." She nodded toward the yarn. "And that romance book isn't your genre."

"I see." He laughed. "It really does look like a woman lives here." He pulled the woolen tangle from the basket. "Orion's teaching me to knit. I think she worries about me being alone and the lessons are an excuse to spend time over here. She's having me start by knitting a square. It's harder than you think."

"I've never tried it," she said. "Looks terribly time consuming." She lifted the paperback. "And this?"

"Guilty. Dimphy left it here, but out of a disjointed sense of curiosity, I started reading it."

"How do you like it so far?" She smiled.

"I'm pretty sure I've got the ending figured out, happily ever after. But I do have one question." She raised her eyebrows. "Why did women where corsets? And how is it that Dimphy still sells them today?"

"To look attractive to men?" She laughed. "Reading and knitting, any other hobbies?"

"I work out with the guys at the firehouse gym pretty regularly. It's one of the quirks of being an EMT. That, and they support a lot of the causes on the island. Did you notice the tree I set up at the store?"

"Yes, I saw it, sitting right inside the front door."

"We hang the names of families who could use a hand this Christmas. Meals, household items, toys for the kids. I worked with Father O'Brian and we came up with a list. The tree is bare now. Shoppers took all the tags and agreed to sponsor the family listed."

Annie tried not to think of the expensive meal she would enjoy with her family, the extent of the holiday celebration. They would sit around an elegantly decorated table and pass small packages to each other. Had they ever given to charity beyond bumping up the check that went in the basket on Christmas Eve? She couldn't even tell you the name of anyone in need.

In New York her circle was executives and vice presidents. She walked by homeless people every day on the way to Global World Bank. Often times they were bundled up in threadbare garments and worn blankets. She just assumed someone was taking care of them. Wasn't there a soup kitchen or something?

"I'm sure my little tree at the store looks like a small effort compared to what you can accomplish from Wall Street." He stood and took the now empty mugs and board.

Annie tried not to change her facial expression. It was as if he'd read her thoughts and was taking her to task. Her office passed around an envelope each year collecting donations to send to... what was it? Just last week she had dug through her purse and cheerfully handed over her cash. Well, as happily as she could be, having been interrupted during her work day.

"About that dinner, are you up for it?" he asked.

Annie raised her left hand and the stone caught the sunlight. "Engaged, remember?"

"That's a fine diamond." He opened the front door. "But until I see a wedding band, I'm still in this game."

Chapter Nine

"How's she doing?" Annie and Menno whispered as they entered Greet's home.

"See for yourself." Greet motioned toward Nel who sat on the floor. "How can I ever thank you? I was so scared. I reacted just the opposite of you and couldn't move. I was frozen. Thank God you were there."

"Aunt Annie!" The young girl jumped up and ran to hug her aunt. "You pulled me out of the water." She looked up at her hero. "Dresses aren't made for in the ocean."

"You got that right." Annie smiled, filled with a sense of relief. "I've just stopped in to get some clothes. Menno and I are going to dinner if you'd like to join us."

"Can we go mom? Please?"

"Sorry Nel, but that's a hard no," Greet said. "These two grown-ups deserve some well-earned alone time."

Menno took a seat on the sofa while Annie flew up the stairs and into the guest bedroom. She held up the few shirts and dresses she had packed and searched for the most casual. Menno would appreciate having a bite to eat with the old Annie. What she found was nothing like she imagined. Her stiff button-downs and narrow legged slacks suddenly looked stuffy and presumptuous.

She yelled down the stairs, "Greet, may I borrow an outfit?"

Having been given permission, she went into Greet's room. Bingo. Summer tops and colorful dresses filled the closet and drawers. As she began perusing, her cell buzzed.

"Stewart, hello. I wasn't expecting your call." She held a bright ruffled top up to her chin and looked in the mirror.

"I'm on the subway and thought I might catch you," he said. "I got your text with the new flight information. I just wanted to double check on your arrival time tomorrow and offer to pick you up at LaGuardia."

Annie stared at herself in the mirror. Her complexion was showing the effect of the island sun and her eyes shone from her tanned skin. Her hair tumbled in soft waves past her shoulders and naturally framed her face. She wasn't exactly looking at a stranger, although the argument could be made, but she was seeing herself the way she once was. Annie from the past looked back at her and a grin crept across her lips. This Annie looked genuinely happy.

"I'm sorry, what about tomorrow?" she asked.

"Save the cab fee," Steward said. "I'll pick you up at the airport. Still landing at noon?"

Tomorrow at noon? That seemed too soon. It felt as though she'd just gotten here. She put the top back in the dresser. When she booked the flight, she was sure she'd have this marriage fixed and little Nel on her good side again. She'd extended the stay by a day, but she was just now getting to see everyone. She'd hardly had time to talk with Corrie and now, Menno. She wasn't ready to leave quite yet.

"Actually, I've extended my stay again." The lie poured easily. "Just one more day." When he didn't respond, she added, "Things are worse with Greet and Puck than I originally thought."

"I hadn't realized that," he said. "Okay then, one more day. Text me the new flight information, the offer to pick you up still stands. Take care."

"Goodbye Stewart." She looked at her screen then remembered something. "Oh! I love—" But he was gone.

She found that top again and matched it with a flowing skirt from the closet. Once dressed, she slipped her feet into a pair of Greet's pretty blue sandals. She returned to her room and found her wallet. All these flight changes were starting to add up. After accessing the airline's website, she paid a hefty fee and changed her travel dates once again. She made a mental note to send Stewart the arrival time later. The conversation with her fiancé already forgotten, Annie put the phone on the nightstand and headed downstairs.

"I don't want to interfere with your plans," Greet said. "But my mom knows you're here and insists on a visit. Any chance on meeting up at her place this evening? Menno, you're invited too. Mom still bakes those cutout sugar cookies. Dozens of snowmen and stars need to be eaten."

"I'll help." Nel said.

"I'd love to see her," Annie said. "We'll text you when we're on our way."

They followed the road south along the oceanfront until Menno slowed the truck and pulled into Tu Amo Beach.

"No way!" Annie threw her hands in the air. "The Kite City food truck? I can't believe it."

"It's nice to know some things never change," he said. "This was always your favorite."

Kite City's red and white flag flapped over the truck alerting passersby they were open for business. Menno parked in the gravel lot near the old bread truck that had found a second life. The new owners painted it white and stenciled *Kite City* on both sides. Under the name they placed their motto; *Kite-Drink-Eat-Relax* reminding the public what their priorities should be.

People were milling about, either enjoying their meal or waiting for their order. A good sized crowd laid about the beach, some watching their children splash in the surf, others catching the last rays of the day. Annie and Menno climbed the three steps to the window. She half expected to see the man who originally owned the business. She couldn't recall his name but he had made his living at sea until a mast gave way in a storm. He ended up with a permanent limp. But it was a younger woman who smiled at them from the opening. She and the two men cooking behind her all wore red Santa hats.

"Merry Christmas, Menno," she said. "What looks good to you today?"

"Oh, it all looks good," he said. "What's the fresh catch?"

Hearing Menno's question, Annie felt her smile slip. It once was her own father who used to provide the fish here. She would ride shot gun with him after he returned from his work on the water. The special that day would be whatever was biting. Carrying a couple of large tuna one day and a cooler full of barracuda or lionfish the next, her dad delivered them fresh from the ocean.

They each ordered the blackened tuna steak with rice and the local beer. They sat at a temporary card table set up on the stone lot. Above them two retired kite sails flapped in the onshore breeze and provided limited shade. The sun was sinking to the horizon casting paint strokes of reds and yellows across the sky. Where the rays touched the ocean, colors poured like silk across the water.

Menno cracked open the cans and slid one over the table. He held his up. "Let's drink to many more days together on Tu Amo Beach."

Annie touched her can to his and took a long refreshing drink. She wiped her mouth with the back of her hand. "I don't know about the *many more* part. I'm still expected home for Christmas."

"This *is* your home. You *are* home for Christmas."

"What do you think, I can just pitch my life and hang out on the beach with you? I have responsibilities, a good job that I worked very hard to get and a family whose counting on me."

"Define good job."

She let out a chuckle. "Okay Mr. Webster, definition of a good job. It's... I'd say it's... I make pretty good money. Not enough to buy my own home in the city yet, but they're dangling a nice pay increase in front of me. There's room for advancement, so I'm always motivated to do my best work. I'm in charge of a small team. Granted, they're not all as driven as I am but they're good at following directions. My goals are concrete, no guessing what the objectives are. I get to crunch numbers and influence important decisions. Sure, the hours are long and sometimes grueling, and I can't remember the last true vacation I took. But, in the end, it's..." She took a moment. "It's—"

"It's what you want and makes you happy." He finished her thought, challenging her to agree.

"I, yes, of course. It's what I've always worked toward." She took a long drink.

"Why investment banking?"

"It was my uncle's career. I think I wanted to make him—"

"Proud of you?"

"Not so much proud of me. I didn't want him to regret having to raise me." There it was. The painful truth she'd carried with her all these years. That day ten years ago when she moved into the brownstone, she knew it. Peggy and Joe had been childfree by choice. Their lives, as well as their beautiful home, were never meant to include a teenager. Their living room alone contained so many museum quality furnishings that Annie imagined a red velvet stanchion rope draped across the entryway.

That first day she was shown to what was to become her bedroom. The space was filled with her aunt's things. An easel held an acrylic piece not yet completed. The artist's instruments were neatly lined on a French farm table. An entire wall shelved books with authors such as Jane Austin and Louisa May Alcott. The works of Charles Dickens took up an entire row. In the corner a Victorian lounge upholstered in a gold fleur de lis had a warm throw tossed at the foot.

With her aunt firmly imprinted in this room, Annie rolled her two suitcases inside and couldn't imagine how this was going to work.

"They gave up the life they had planned for themselves to take me in. They were nothing but wonderful to me. I've always bent over backward to be easy and good. The perfect daughter they never wanted."

Annie remembered sleeping on the pretty lounge just one night. The next day movers and delivery men swarmed the house like a colony of ants. By her second night in her new home, the room had morphed into something a seventeen year old would feel comfortable in.

She had placed a framed photo of her and her parents on the dresser. Happier times. In the image, the three sat at a table, each with an entire red lobster in front of them. They held a cracker in one hand and a pick in the other, laughing as the photo was taken. She remembered that day, not so long ago. She and her father had gone scuba diving, with the goal of a seafood dinner for three on their minds.

Thankfully, the bookshelf filled with yet to be discovered tales remained in her new room. The novels offered her a blissful escape as she learned how to cope in the city. She became an avid reader and an honorary member of Aunt Peggy's book club.

"I can't just leave my aunt and uncle after all they've done for me. I love them. I want them to see that I've succeeded. They have to know that their sacrifice was worth it, that they produced a successful, happy individual with a bright future. That's what I am."

"I'm sorry Annie. I knew it was hard on you, but I never understood to what extent. You talk about how this island takes care of their own. But we failed you and let you be taken from us."

"It was out of everyone's hands."

"Not everyone's." He stiffened. "There is one person who could've prevented all of this from happening to you, to us."

"I don't blame him." She reached across the table and put her fingertips on the back of his hand. "He was suffering along with me."

Menno took her hand in both of his. "Will you answer one more question for me?"

"Sure."

"What's your fiancé's name? Because, for all the reasons you just gave me why you need to return to New York, he never came up."

———

Greet's mother threw open the door causing the tinsel wreath to sway. "Welcome home!" The emotion on her face warmed Annie's heart. When she lunged forward and wrapped her in her arms, it was all either woman could do to calm the tears that flowed.

"It's wonderful to see you again." Annie's words were mumbled in the crook of the woman's neck. She held her mother's best friend like she might float away. The longer they embraced, the heavier the stream of tears became and soon Annie stopped fighting and allowed her sobs to gush.

Maud had been as much a mother to her as her own. Greet and Annie were raised as sisters because their mothers considered themselves that close. All her young life Annie freely ran in and out of this home. So often, that she had kept a drawer of clothes and a toothbrush here. She spent countless nights sleeping on the trundle bed in Greet's room. Maud would call Annie's mom and simply say, "I got her."

"Let me look at my Annie." Maud held her at arm's length. "You've become a beautiful woman. I truly believe you were sent here to save my granddaughter today. My soul is dancing now that you've come home."

"I'm a blubbering mess." Annie wiped at her tears but couldn't take her eyes off Maud. She'd grown a little plump, and grey hair now dotted her temples, but her warm and caring spirit was unchanged.

"Menno," Maud said. "I'm so glad you could come. It's just like old times around here. Please, come inside." She stepped aside and held the door. "Greet and Nel are in the back room. Menno, why don't you go join them. I'd like some time with my second daughter if you don't mind."

"Of course." He glanced at Annie and paused, after just a moment, he left the room.

"Sit Annie, please." Maud motioned toward the sofa. "There are some sugar cookies there on the plate. Help yourself." She disappeared into the kitchen. Annie had eaten three by the time she returned with a tea set. She placed it on the coffee table and dropped bags into two cups. "This was your mother's favorite."

"Mandarin orange," Annie said, her tears now slowing.

"With a—"

"Cinnamon stick," she said, sniffling.

"Exactly." Maud placed the delicate teacups on china saucers and handed one to her. She sat and held her own. "I like to think Rose is here with me when I fix her favorite tea. Especially this time of year when the orange and cinnamon help to warm me."

"It really does taste like the holiday," Annie said. "My Aunt Peggy makes a hot spiced wine when the evenings get cold. She adds cloves and a splash of brandy to a bottle of Merlot and lets it heat on the stove. The aroma fills the entire kitchen."

"I'll have to try it," Maud said. "When your mom first found out she was sick, she showed up here with a bottle of wine. Was it Merlot?" She tried to remember. "Well, I'm sure it was red. She came in and found two of my finest stemmed glasses. Here I thought we were celebrating something." Her mood turned bleak. "She poured and handed one to me. We held them up and I asked her, 'What are we toasting to?' and Rose said, 'To a life well lived.' We sat together right there on that sofa and she explained it was her own life we needed to celebrate." She blinked away tears and looked into her tea.

"That sounds like my mom. She was so strong through the entire thing. Even when the treatments became worse than the illness, she just kept on pushing."

"She was a tough one all right," Maud said. "Who else wouldn't notice any symptoms until they were in stage four? Maybe she did and chose to ignore them, I don't know. Her life was so full of her volunteer work and teaching and raising you. I imagine she just had more important things to do than worry about an ache or pain."

"I don't think I ever thanked you," Annie said. "For sitting with her when my dad couldn't."

"Men aren't made out for the hard stuff. Not like us women are. We were born with the strength to move forward when everyone else can only stand still. Your dad loved her so much."

"He did. She brought out the best in him."

"Over the course of their marriage they grew inseparable. Like two people made into one. He couldn't watch her die. It would've been like seeing his own spirit being ripped from his very chest."

"He hated to feel so helpless," Annie said. "For such a strong man, he'd finally met his match. I've always wondered if he had faced losing her, would he have been able to move on?"

"We'll never know," Maud said. "I do know that your father lost a big part of himself that day. Pieces that would never be found again. You have that same heart,

it's what brought you back to us. You love Greet like a sister and you're here for her. Her heart is broken. Talking to me is one thing but having you for support and advice is a true blessing."

"I'm sorry it's taken me so long to return. When Greet told me your husband died, I tried—" She stumbled over her weak excuse. "I wanted to come, but—" What was it that kept her from attending his funeral? "Lee was like a father to me, I'm sorry for your loss."

"Thank you, that's kind of you to say. I don't know what I would've done without Greet."

"Speaking of Greet, I should go say hello." She began gathering her cup and saucer when Maud's hand touched hers.

"I wanted to tell you one thing before we join them," Maud said. Annie set the china down again. "Your mother left me a gift. It's in the other room and I don't want to upset you." She stood and put her hand out. "Come with me."

Chapter Ten

A nnie followed Maud to the family room. Unlike the more formal sitting space, this was where everyday life occurred. The dark paneled walls from the 1970's remained. They somehow made the room feel warm instead of outdated. Garland was strung over the windows and a six foot tree blinked on and off. Gifts wrapped in red and green sat underneath it and a gold star shone at the top. On the television, a strange green character was stealing Christmas, yet to be washed in the true meaning of the holiday. Nel and Greet snuggled under a blanket with their eyes on the screen. Flames crackled in the fireplace and pleasantly warmed the cozy room.

"Aunt Annie!" Nel threw off the comforter and ran to her. She wrapped her little arms around her aunt's waist. "You're here."

"I am. I had a nice visit with your Grandmother." Annie returned the hug and kissed the top of her head. She wondered at the fact that simply being here could elicit such a response.

Menno stood and watched Annie expectantly. She nodded at him and then scanned the room. Like a child hunting for the elf on the shelf, she searched for what it was Maud wanted her to see. Her

106

eyes landed on the fireplace. She was hardly aware of Menno taking her hand.

The mantel was covered in snowy fabric with tiny lights woven throughout. An entire town sat quietly on the frosted grounds. A mix of buildings that looked suspiciously like Kralendijk. Miniscule green wreaths with red bows hung on the front doors. In the windows of two, candlesticks glowed. All the rooftops were covered in new fallen snow. A white light shone steady at the top of Willemstoren light-house. Nearby, a yellow church with a steeple reaching to the sky sat next to a matching bell tower. Greenery adorned with purple bows and strings of garland looped a top the windows. San Bernardo Church.

Annie squeezed Menno's hand and stepped closer to the Christmas village. A shining red barn with bales of hay stacked out front was positioned next to a field of pine trees. On the hearth were even more homes, a skating rink, and a toy shop. Elves created dolls and trucks, all in various stages of completion. Santa's sleigh was filled and ready for takeoff. Eight tiny reindeer waited for the signal to fly.

The village was a testament to its creator. Looking closely, one could appreciate the details that went into its formation. Every wreath that hung on a door not only had a bow, but a wire that hung from a tiny nail. Annie remembered her mother's fingers as they tapped the metal piece into a door.

If she peered inside the barn, she knew that her favorite reindeer would be resting in the hay, his nose shining red. And underneath the church, her mother had written the date the original building was constructed. She made a dash and recorded the date she completed her miniature version. With just a bit of imagination, if one looked closely at the doll an elf was carrying, Annie's young face was looking back at you. Or so her mother had told her.

"There are seventeen figures," Annie said. "She made one each fall beginning the year I was born." She placed her finger on an evergreen tree that stood above the others. She remembered her mother using a glue gun to attached dried greens on a cone shaped foam.

"I hope it's alright," Maud said. "I put her village out each Christmas. I think of Rose as I unwrap the pieces and place them on the mantel. I'd understand if you wanted it for yourself. You'll be married soon and have your own home to display it in."

"Oh, no. My mom wanted you to have it," Annie said. She imagined the handcrafted Christmas village in her aunt's home. For a moment she felt sad knowing her mother's labor of love wouldn't fit in with the holiday décor in her home in New York. "It feels right that it's here with you." She picked up the skating rink. "These two skaters." She pointed to the figures gliding across the ice with their arms interlaced. "Mom said these were you and her. Something about a hole in your jeans."

"Oh heavens." Maud took the figurine and studied it. "I always thought this tear in the fabric came with age." She touched the rip in the pant of one of the skaters. "I can't believe she did this. It's been right here in front of me all these years and I didn't see her message."

"Her message?" Annie asked.

"Your mama and I had just left the Drunken Mermaid," Maud recalled the day.

"Oh, my gosh." Greet sat up straight. "I've got to hear a story that begins with that line."

"We might have had one too many, but we were walking, not driving. We were still new friends, mid-twenties at the time. This was the summer that Rose was volunteering with Dolphin Track. I remember thinking how much I was going to miss her when she returned home to the states. She and Tak hadn't fallen in love yet, or so I thought."

"What's this have to do with the torn pants, mom?" Greet asked.

"We walked down to the wharf to watch the fishing boats come in. One docked and had a big crate of lobsters on the deck. The crew all came ashore and went to speak to the foreman. Rose dared me to snatch a lobster from their catch."

"You did not." Greet grinned.

"She thought we should set one free." Maud giggled and threw her hand up. "Don't ask me where my head was, it might've been the tequila doing the thinking, but sure enough I climbed on the boat and snatched the largest one I saw. Just as my foot landed back on the dock a crazy dog came barreling out of the wheelhouse hell bent on catching me."

"Mom! You were a hellion!" Greet laughed.

"Not a very good one," Maud said. "That dog grabbed me by the seat of my pants and wouldn't let go." She laughed as she remembered. "I dropped that lobster like a hot potato and luckily the dog cowered away. Rose and I ran like the devil. We'd made it to the church before we stopped to catch our breath. She said we should slow down so we wouldn't look guilty. We walked through town heading for home. She started laughing and asked me, 'does it feel a little breezy Maud?' I didn't know what that girl was talking about. People kept staring at us. I thought they all knew about the attempted lobster kidnapping." She laughed and tears filled her eyes. "Turned out, that dog kept a very large piece of my britches. My bare bottom was on full display."

"Oh, mom, you didn't."

Maud studied the skater with the hole ripped in her backside. "Oh, Rose, boy do I miss you."

A knock at the door had Nel running to open it. "Daddy's here!"

Greet stiffened. "Puck's taking Nel to the showing of *My Dog Frosty*. We haven't worked out any formal arrangements yet. I guess that'll come with time."

Nel held her father's hand and pulled him into the family room. Puck glanced at the crowd then fist-bumped Menno. "Hey man, good to see you. Annie, you're still here. I thought you were heading home today."

"I was," Annie said. "I've postponed my flight."

"Hello Greet." Puck looked to the floor and clasped his hands behind his back.

"Nel honey," Greet said. "Go grab your bag and say goodbye to grandma." The young girl scuttled out of the room. "Puck, we need to talk about Christmas," Greet said once Nel was out of earshot. "I don't want Nel juggled around between us."

"Whatever you want to do is fine with me."

"What I want is for you to *care* about what we do." She left the room but not before Annie saw her tears pooling.

"I do care," Puck whispered. "She's wrong about that."

Annie had seen some break ups in her lifetime. Short and long term relationships that had once flew high crashed and burned. Usually it was one, but sometimes both parties involved that believed they were the one wronged. Once loving people turned against one another and things got ugly.

But this wasn't what she was seeing between her friends. Neither acted angry or full of rage or seemed to hold any ill will against the other. On the contrary, they looked like a pair of worn dishrags that had been hung out to dry. She'd expected resentment or to witness heated arguments between them. But since arriving on Bonaire, she'd not seen any of that.

"Puck," Annie said. "I've extended my stay because I haven't accomplished what I came here for. I mean to be supporting my best friend but I'm having a hard time understanding what's going on between you two."

"I'm ready Daddy." Nel came in with her jacket on.

"Can we get together tomorrow?" Annie asked. "How about a coffee before you leave for work?"

"That sounds nice," he said. "If sevens not too early, I can meet you at the Bon Air Café."

"Perfect."

"I think I'll head out with Puck and Nel," Menno said. "I've kept you all to myself this afternoon. I want to be sure you have plenty of time with Greet and Maud."

"Thanks, that's very thoughtful." She walked to the front door and saw them all off. She called, "Have fun at the movie."

"I will!" Nel skipped at the end of her father's hand.

"You girls sit and enjoy that fire," Maud said. "I'm going to make some hot chocolate."

"Thanks mom." Greet sat on a comfortable upholstered arm chair near the hearth. Annie took the twin on the opposite side. The warm home and sounds from Maud moving about the kitchen had them feeling like kids again.

"I don't mean to bring up a sore subject," Annie said. "But honestly, I feel as though something is going on here that I'm missing. Did you see how shy Puck was acting around you? That man isn't showing the signs of someone who wants to be single."

"Maybe his new girlfriend left him." Her face went pale.

"You don't know he has a new girl, you said so yourself. I did a little snooping and Menno hasn't seen any signs of another woman. The question is, why would a man, who clearly loves his wife, leave her?"

"That's the question all right, the sixty -four-thousand dollar question." Greet kicked off her shoes and shifted in the chair.

"Whatever it is, I plan to get to the bottom of it."

"I hope you have better luck than I have." She placed her palm on her forehead and drug it back over her hair.

"Do you know what I do for a living?"

"Yes, of course, you're an investment banker."

"I rely on carefully honed verbal skills and relationship building to get what I want." She pointed her thumb at her chest. "I'm a snake in the grass when it comes to convincing uncooperative businesses to do exactly what I want them to. I strike and they sign on the bottom line, never knowing what hit them."

"Lord, Annie, that sounds awful."

"Well, yes, now that I've said it out loud, I can see why you'd say that. The point is, Puck will be putty in my hands."

Annie and Greet sipped from heavy ceramic mugs while Maud busied herself in the kitchen. Pots and pans clanged and cabinet doors opened and closed. Soon, the smell of something wonderful was drifting through the house.

It was inevitable that the two would take a long stroll down memory lane. As they spoke it became clear. Annie's memories were Greet's memories and the realization of this comforted them.

Puck had been right when he and Annie had spoken in the church. Growing up on Bonaire with the best of friends and loving families was special. Something extraordinary that some searched a lifetime for. The island itself nurtured this unique community. At only twenty four miles long and seven miles wide, those who lived within her shoreline were gently coaxed toward living in harmony. They shaped families that escaped the definition and were bound by the land even more so than blood. Fashioning a life where peace was commonplace and no one would think to destroy it.

"I wonder what my life would've been like had I stayed," Annie said. "If my father had been strong enough to care for me."

"I'm trying to imagine my life if I'd been moved to New York City." They laughed. "Maybe I'd be an independently wealthy professional with killer clothes and a romantic fiancé."

"What makes you think Stewart's romantic?"

"I'm just guessing. But by the size of that rock on your finger, I'm envisioning Christopher Plummer and Julie Andrews."

"That movie always gets me. When they—"

"Dance in the garden." They said in unison and giggled.

"That was a great love story," Annie said. "You'd do well in the city. Takes a little getting used to, but it has its advantages."

"No having to wait for the next cargo ship to restock the pastry cabinet at the grocery?"

"We do always have plenty of treats. You'd love the theatre and the culture. We'll have to plan for you to come visit me. Now that your—" She caught herself. "We have plenty of room in the brownstone."

"Now that I'm single?" Her face went grey and fell with grief.

"I didn't mean it. I'm sorry. I wasn't thinking, it slipped out." Annie watched as Greet's very essence sank. Her heart had taken on too much water. "Can I tell you something that's going to sound crazy right now?"

"Sure," Greet said. "I don't think anything can shock me anymore."

"I'm jealous of you," Annie said. "I know your heart is breaking even as we speak, but I can't help wanting to know... how it... feels."

"You want everything you thought was true and reliable and certain, stolen away?" She swiped at her eyes. "Too tired to sleep, too hungry to eat. This huge weight on me trying to make life look normal for my daughter. This is what you want to *feel*?"

Annie put her mug on the table and knelt in front of her friend. She took her hands and held them tightly. "To be so in love, the way you feel about Puck. I want to know what it's like to be head over heels in love with someone."

"Oh, Annie." She reached for her and they embraced. "You used to know. Don't you remember?"

———

"You didn't think I'd let you leave without a homecooked meal, did you?" Maud ladled hearty chili into heavy ceramic bowls and placed them on the table.

"Knock, knock." A familiar voice came from the front room. Corrie appeared in the kitchen. "Hi. I saw Menno on my way out of work. He said I might find you all here. Room for one more?"

"There's always room," Maud said, pulling a fourth bowl from the cabinet. "Greet, I've got some beer on the bottom shelf. Grab one for everyone, will you please?"

"And once again," Corrie said. "My timing is perfect."

Like a hive of bees, the four buzzed around the kitchen. Corrie found beer mugs and Greet popped the tops and poured. Annie went straight to the utensil drawer and found spoons and napkins then placed them around the table.

"You girls sit," Maud said. "I'll get the bread out of the oven."

"This is wonderful, thank you," Annie said. The smell of the fresh baked rolls had her mouth watering. Maud placed a basket on the table. Perfectly executed, they looked like a sunrise over a mound of soft butter. "You really shouldn't have gone to the trouble." She tore open a hot roll.

"This was no work at all. I'm just so happy to see you girls together again."

Annie dipped the bread into her bowl catching small bits of beef and chunks of tomato. It smelled of love and home and as it melted in her mouth, she couldn't remember anything ever tasting so delicious.

Maud sat next to her and took her hand. She then clasped Greet's and she in turn found Corrie's. They closed their eyes and bowed their heads.

Mortified, Annie put the remains of the roll in her bowl, quickly wiped her hand on the napkin and took Corrie's free hand.

Maud said a prayer of thanks for the bounty set before them. She added, "We are blessed with all that is good as the angels have brought our family together again. Amen."

"Amen," they said in unison.

Maud became animated as she tried to catch Annie up on all the events she'd missed. Greet pointed out it would take a month of Sundays to cover all that had happened on Bonaire in the last ten years. Her mother was not dissuaded and continued with the telling of what could only be described as a real life soap opera. "You remember Francine. She was in your high school class until her mother decided to homeschool her. Well, she was getting an education all right."

"Mom." Greet warned. "Don't."

"Greet, let her tell it." Corrie said.

"An education?" Annie prodded. Being privy to the local chat, she felt like one of the girls. Sitting here, surrounded by friends, she began to understand what all the hype was about. She now appreciated what she'd been missing out on all these years.

"Turned out she was," Maud whispered, "pregnant. And the daddy wasn't a student, if you know what I mean. Her mother worried what it would do to her," she made air quotes, "high stature in the community. The family decided to send her to Columbia to have her baby."

"Mom, stop. This is just ugly gossip."

"It's not gossip when it's true, dear."

"She's right," Corrie egged on. "It's not gossip if it's the truth. Go on Miss Maud."

"Can you imagine that? Sending your own daughter away?"

"Please, stop." Greet rolled her eyes but Annie couldn't stifle her giggle.

"She came back a year later claiming she'd adopted this beautiful little boy." Maud took a long drink of her beer. "And everyone just walked around like we believed that story. The entire island was acting like an ostrich with its head stuck in the sand and pretending to enjoy the view."

"Did we ever find out who the father was?" Annie's curiosity was getting the best of her. No matter the subject, she wanted this evening to last forever. What was it her assistant Virginia called it? Her tribe. Annie was with her tribe and she couldn't imagine a better place to be.

"Do you remember that man who used to sell watermelons out of the back of his truck?"

"Mother."

"I always thought that kid looked familiar." Corrie said.

"At least when Greet was expecting I didn't try to hide it to save my reputation."

"Are we really going there?" Greet asked.

"I was so happy to have a grand one on the way. I ran out and bought a crib and diapers. There would be no hiding the miracle of life in this family."

"The end." Greet said. "Can we move on, please?"

They finished the tasty chili using their rolls to sop up the last of it until the bowls were empty. When they were done, each helped clear and got the dishes sorted. Once the kitchen was back in order, they moved to the family room. The fire was smoldering but Corrie fed it small pieces and got it burning again.

"Father O'Brian asked me if I'd sing soloist on Christmas Eve," Greet said. "Silvia's daughter is taking her to Paris for the holiday."

"Oh Greet," Maud said. "How wonderful. You've always enjoyed singing in the choir. Now's your time to shine. Your voice was made to sing soloist."

"I told him I couldn't do it. I just can't bring myself to feel any joy. Pretending I have the Christmas spirit for Nel is difficult enough. I'd never be able to belt out *O Holy Night*. It's such a beautiful hymn, but just thinking about those lyrics brings me to tears."

"I wish there was something I could do to make this all go away," Corrie said.

"Maybe if you take some baby steps," Maud said. "Something to take your mind off of all your troubles. You were talking about going back to school. Why don't you and Nel move in here with me? I can help take care of my granddaughter and you can study."

"Thanks mom, but I don't have the motivation anymore. Originally, I thought if I could get a better paying job, Puck wouldn't have to work so hard with the department of transportation. He always thought he would move up the ranks there, but all these years later, he's still repairing potholes."

"He has such a tough job, that man is a hard worker."

"I thought about registering for the IT Systems program at the vocational school. When I mentioned it to him, he said he always wanted to take the electrical technician courses there." She dabbed her eyes with her napkin. "Then we got into a fight over who should go back to school and how will we pay the rent. It was awful. He left me shortly after that. I've lost everything."

"I'm not so sure about that," Annie said. "Unless I'm way off. I don't see Puck doing a complete one eighty from the days I knew him. He was always such a great guy, and I'm pretty sure he still is. This can't be what he wants. From what I'm seeing every indication says he still loves you. Don't give up just yet. Remember, it's Christmas, a time for miracles."

———

They were enjoying the fire when they heard a knock at the door. Someone let themselves in and closed the door behind them.

"Corrie already let herself in," Greet said. "Let's see who this is. I've got five dollars on… Menno!" She winked at her friends as he entered the room. "What a pleasant surprise."

"I hope I'm not interrupting anything," he said. "I thought I'd offer to walk Annie home."

"How noble of you," Corrie said. "Who knows what kind of hoodlums she might run into."

"Let's let them decide who's walking where with whom." Maud directed Corrie into the kitchen and Greet disappeared with them.

"So subtle." A smile grew over Annie's face and she felt her heart speed up at the sight of him. She inhaled and tried to control the blush she felt creeping up her neck.

"We could stop by the chocolate shop on the way. They're making nutmeg truffles for the holiday season."

"That sounds delicious, I'd love to try them. Do you mind if we go by Greet's first? I'd like to put on a jacket."

"Sure."

"Let me just say goodbye."

"I'll wait for you out front."

Annie fell into Maud's arms and promised to stop by again before she left the island. Maud handed her a brown paper bag with sugar cookies "for the road" piled inside. Corrie and Greet were going to stay and watch Christmas movies on their favorite channel.

"Ready to go," Annie pulled the door closed behind her.

They followed the sidewalk then turned in the direction of Greet's home. The air was chilly and Menno apologized for not having a coat to offer her.

"I'm fine, it's only a short walk. This is actually balmy compared to New York. We're covered in snow up there. And our blizzards aren't conveniently confined to the town square."

"In a way Bonaire is like our very own Camelot. We have the good fortune of sitting south of the hurricane belt and holding a steady eighty-two degrees most days. Sure, the nights are getting cooler, but it is December after all." He motioned. "Turn here."

The sun was setting and the streets were quiet. Lights were coming on inside the homes they passed. Annie reached into the bag and offered Menno a star shaped cookie. She fished one out for herself and three bites later they were searching for another.

"No more emergency calls from your boss?" he asked, then took a bite.

Annie patted her hips and bottom searching for her cell. "Wow. I've been without my phone all day. I haven't even missed it." She stopped. "I know this is supposed to be a good thing, but I'm about to freak out. Where is it?" She began to retrace her steps. She had spoken to Stewart, but that was early this morning. Then she remembered changing her flight and answering text messages. "I left it at Greet's place hours ago. That's so unlike me. I'm not usually forgetful."

"Take a breath, we'll be there soon. Any messages will still be waiting."

"But what if—" She thought of Richard.

"No worrying. Nothing can be so important that you give yourself anxiety over it."

They walked along the side of the street and the sky morphed from a burnt orange glow to a soft flamingo pink. Wispy clouds drifted across the falling sun. They made two more turns, each time Menno having to direct her.

"I used to know these streets like my daily commute on the

subway." She studied the houses around her. "Wait. Isn't this..." She stopped in front of a modest one story home. Her first thought was that the structure had shrunken. It seemed quite expansive all her young life. Regardless of its size, this house she knew. The door was smack dab in the center and behind the window to the left was the kitchen. She could almost see her mother washing dishes there. On the right side, a glow from the fireplace danced behind the sheer curtains.

"Should we knock?" Menno asked in a whisper. "I'm sure you'd like to see inside."

"I can already see inside." She spoke in a hush, imagining her father in his oversized easy chair after a long day. He'd pat his lap and her mother would snuggle up with him. They were embarrassingly in love, even after almost twenty years of marriage and one daughter between them.

Annie's bedroom had faced the backyard. An elderly couple, Mr. and Mrs. Clarke, lived quietly in the house behind theirs for as long as she could remember. She used to watch them out her window. Often time, during particularly hot evenings, they would sit on their back deck. He read large novels and she worked with her colorful needlecraft. How many times had Annie accidentally sent her soccer ball flying into their yard? While retrieving it, she could always expect a wave from Mrs. Clarke and an invitation to come inside for a cool drink.

At one time Annie's room was lined with posters of her favorite TV stars and pop rock bands. The walls later were painted a pretty shade of lilac. She could still hear the music they listened to while she and her mother went up and down a ladder with brushes dripping. *Annie this color is almost as beautiful as you,* her mother had said.

She could still see her father tinkering under the hood of his car and tending to the vegetable garden. As the physical labors of his job began taking a toll on his back, he enlisted Menno to help build raised beds. They must've been fourteen or fifteen at the time, their hearts stirring and ultimately shifting them from childhood friends to teenagers in love.

Annie took his hand as she remembered thanking God for Menno. He was her support while her mom's health failed and her father sank into nothingness. Not wanting her to pass in the cold hospital, they made her as comfortable as they could in this little house. The day before she died, she asked to be moved from her bed to the sofa in the main room. Her dad moved pillows and quilts and created a cozy nest to lay her in. She was light as a feather and he had no trouble carrying her and resting her among the billowy fabrics.

Annie's heart broke as she watched him gather her favorite things and place them on the coffee table for her to enjoy. Photos of her parents and extended family members. Pictures of trips they had taken together. A stuffed teddy bear her grandmother had given her as a child. A portrait of the two of them standing on the beach. She wore a brilliant white dress and he a tuxedo.

I'm sorry. Her mother had said. *I never thought death would part us so soon.*

"You're crying." Menno put his arm around her and she placed her cheek against his chest.

A shadow moved about in the kitchen then stood at the sink below the window. The fluorescent bulb lighting him and making him visible from the street. He pushed his dark hair off his face, exposing the scar that had disfigured him since childhood.

"Daddy," Annie said in a breath.

Chapter Eleven

They watched Tak, Annie's father, as his shadow moved from room to room. She recalled the story of how her parents met. "My mom was on Bonaire for the summer. She had graduated college but couldn't quite settle down. She'd taken a volunteer position with a wildlife group here. As she told it to me, she was down at the wharf and asked the longshoreman if anyone with a boat was available to run her over to the islet off the coast. He pointed at Tak, but my dad didn't want to be seen by such a pretty girl and he tried to act busy."

"I can't imagine how a disfigurement like that might effect someone's life."

"I've told him a million times that a scar can't make him less of a person," Annie said. "I was little when I realized there was something different about his face. Mom told me that when dad was just seven years old, he went fishing with his father. They loved their time on the boat and spent most weekends with their lines in the water. One day his father struggled with the grappling anchor. It was hung up on something just below the surface. My dad leaned over the side just as the anchor broke free, came out of the water, drug over his face and sank into his cheek."

"That's terrible," Menno said. "He was so young I'm surprised it didn't kill him. I'm sure your grandfather must've panicked."

"He rushed him to the hospital, but after all the treatment, he was left with only partial sight in the damaged eye and a contorted face and lip. It was different back then. His mother kept him out of school. She thought she was doing the right thing, safeguarding her son from the other kids. She didn't want to see him teased or hurt."

"So, your dad never got a formal education?" Menno asked.

"She taught him at home," Annie said. "Just basic math and reading. She thought she was protecting him but all she was doing was enforcing his belief that the scar made him less than everyone else. I know Grandma was trying, but she didn't do him any favors. As he grew older, he became a recluse. The scar spread and moved inside of him, resting deep in his heart."

The light in the kitchen went out and the porch light came to life.

"When his father died, he went to work at the wharf. It's all he was qualified to do."

"And that's where he met your mother?"

"He told me it was the first time a stranger spoke to him without staring or jumping back with fright. My mom looked at him as though there were no scars at all."

"I can see that about your mother," Menno said. "She was the most kind-hearted person on this island."

"My dad's life changed when he was with her. She introduced him to her friends, went to parties and learned to enjoy other people's company, all because of Rose. To hear my father tell it, it was truly a beauty and her beast story."

"A story like that should end happily ever after."

"It certainly should have, don't you think? As she neared her end she asked to be moved to the sofa. She didn't want to pass in the bed she knew my father would sleep alone in for the rest of his life."

"Make yourself at home," Annie said, as they entered Greet's house. "I'm going to run upstairs, check my cell, and grab a coat." Knowing that what she had packed was limited, she helped herself to Greet's jean jacket that was hanging in her closet. She stopped in the guest room and found her cell right where she had left it, on the bedside table next to the seashells. She sat on the comforter and woke up the screen. Listed were two texts, one missed call and a voice message. She touched the first text.

Richard: *Just wanted 2 t u again. We're all set on this end. Merry Xmas.* He had added a thumbs up emoji, a phew emoji and a Christmas tree emoji.

"Thank goodness that got straightened out." She opened the next one.

Stewart: *Don't forget to send me your new arrival information.*

"Oh, dang, the new flight." She went and yelled down the stairs, "Give me a few minutes, I need to text Stewart my arrival information."

"Why don't you stay through the new year?" Menno appeared at the foot of the stairs. "Have Christmas here. We all want you to stay. I want you to stay."

"Didn't we already have this conversation? My family is expecting me. Aunt Peggy made a reservation. Stewart's parents are in Europe, I can't leave him alone."

"I don't remember you being so hard-headed."

"Wrong description. Reliable would be more accurate."

"I'm sorry, you're right. I just hate to see you go so soon." He visibly inhaled and gazed up at her. "Do what you have to, we can leave for the chocolate shop when you're ready."

Annie returned to the room and sat on the bed. She opened and played the voice mail.

Aunt Peggy: *"Hi Annie it's your Aunt Peggy. Stewart tells me you're not coming home tomorrow. I wanted to check that everything's okay there. We miss you. The house is so quiet. Go ahead and stay another day but no longer than that. Okay, love you, bye."*

She wanted to call her back but worried that conversation could get long, so instead, she sent a text.

Annie: *Got your message, everything here is fine. More than fine. I'd forgotten Bonaire is a tropical paradise. Seeing old friends and visiting places I remember from before. Will talk soon. Love to you and Uncle Joe.* She added a heart emoji and touched Send.

"Ready?" Menno stood. "I see you found Greet's jacket. It looks nice on you."

As they walked into town Annie felt something prickling at her insides. It was just a small detail, nothing really, but it spurred something akin to jealousy. Menno knew Greet's jean jacket. It was silly, but this awareness made her uncomfortable. She'd missed out on such great friendships. Relationships that grew and strengthened even in her absence.

"Everything okay?" Menno asked. "You're quiet."

"I'm just thinking," she said, as they approached the center of town, snow now underfoot and flying around them.

"Care to share?"

"I'm wondering," she scooped up a handful of wet flakes, "how an island boy is going to hold up against a Yankee in a snowball fight." She threw the mess at him and it landed square on his chest. She ran a few yards then gathered some more.

"And I'm doubting," Menno said while making one of his own, "that an investment banker will be able to defend herself against the International Caribbean MVP pitcher." He tossed it underhand and it came down on top of her head. "Strike one!"

"I forgot that you were a pitcher." She giggled and packed snow. She heaved it but he ducked and it hit Santa's chair and broke into pieces. "Maybe I shouldn't have started this after all," she said, as a clump of snow landed on her hip. "Uncle! I'm waving the white flag."

"Good idea." He dropped a ball to the ground just as one crashed on his cheek. "Now you've done it." He jogged toward her and picked her up.

"Put me down!" She laughed.

He carried her over his shoulder to the Santa chair. "Time out for you." He gently placed her in it then sat on the arm. They were both out of breath. "You're covered." He mussed her hair trying to free the snow. "That's what you get for starting it. I'm guessing your head is feeling okay."

"Yes, it's fine. I'd even forgotten about the stitches."

They sat as a torrent of flakes blew from the snowmakers on the roofs. The accumulation in the square was approaching two feet. Plenty of signs of children having played in the snow earlier dotted the area around them. A snowman stood wearing a Hawaiian shirt and holding a surfboard. Someone left a red mitten on an icy fort now long abandoned. The owners of the drug store had added lights to the palm trees out front.

"You had today off?" It just occurred to Annie that he hadn't mentioned having to work at the store at all today.

"I went in this morning and worked on payroll. Last year I hired a manager who does a great job. He's able to handle most of the day to day stuff."

"*You* hired a manager?"

"Annie, I own the store, I'm not an employee there."

"Sorry. I misunderstood."

"How about that dessert I promised you?" He stood and held his hand out to her.

"Share a hot chocolate with me?" She took his hand and stood.

"That depends."

"On what?"

"Whipped cream or no whipped cream?"

125

Menno pulled open the door to *Your So Sweets*. The unmistakable smell of cocoa blanketed them as they walked inside. The small shop was a treat for both the eyes and nose. Three display cases encircled the room and bistro style tables crowded the floor. Annie and Menno studied the offerings. Truffles sat on golden trays with pretty calligraphy listing the flavors. Under them, a dozen lines of colorful macaroons tempted anyone who gazed upon them.

Peanuts were trapped in mountains of milk chocolate. Next to them walnuts were encased in the same deliciousness. An entire shelf was dedicated to fresh fruits dipped in white, dark, and milk chocolates.

"It's a tough choice, but I think I'm ready to pick my poison." Annie stood in front of a gleaming glass case. The employee smiled and waited to hear her order. "May I have a raspberry cream, a chocolate covered pretzel," she added, "and a nutmeg truffle." She remembered Menno had mentioned them earlier.

Menno gave his order and the treats were placed in a little white box.

"Is there anything else I can get you?"

"One hot chocolate, please," Menno said.

"With whipped cream or without?"

"With." They chimed in unison.

They sat at one of the wrought iron tables and opened the pretty box. Annie lifted a delicate candy and bit into it. A flood of raspberry and thick cream puddled on her tongue. The chocolate melted and she swirled it around her mouth before swallowing. She took a sip from the mug then wiped the creamy foam from her upper lip. She looked up to see Menno smiling at her.

"Watching you enjoy those makes me feel like I'm doing something illegal."

"This should be against the law it's so good. Thank you for treating me." She put the rest of the candy in her mouth and let out a quiet *yum*.

"I think I owed you one."

"How so?"

"Taking you by your dad's house tonight. I should've gone a different route. I never would purposefully surprise you like that."

"There's no need to apologize. I've been thinking a lot about my father since I got here. I always had so many questions growing up. Early on I thought my uncle was being coy, but as time went by, I realized he didn't have any more answers than I did."

"After your mom died," Menno said. "I wanted to strangle him. I couldn't believe he copped out like that. He gave up on raising you. Just like that he let you go. I went to see him after you'd left."

"You've never told me this."

"I stormed up to his door and let myself in. I was so mad I started to tremble. He was sitting in his recliner in the dark. No television, no lights on. I was so upset they'd moved you away. I screamed, *wake up, wake up and take care of your daughter.* I was awful, so selfish, only thinking of myself."

"I didn't know you did that."

"I'm not proud of my behavior that night." He continued, "Annie, your dad turned to me and the look in his eyes frightened me. He wasn't himself. He was distant, a ghost even. It was as if he were in another place. I couldn't be sure he'd even heard me or knew who I was."

"I worried about how he'd manage without me," Annie said. "He needed me to take care of him, but he didn't see it that way. He and my mom were inseparable and losing her was the end for him. Let's be honest, without my mother, he may not have had any friends or social life to speak of."

"That night, he looked like he was in shock," Menno said. "There was nothing I could do to get him to respond to me."

"I imagine he was sinking back into the recluse he once was. That scar on his face kept him hiding most of his young life. It was mom who brought him out of the shadows and into the light of day. Yes, he loved her, but it was more than that. Every bit of happiness he found was because of her."

"Luckily for your dad," Menno said. "His friends, led by Father O'Brian, weren't going to give up on him. Not like he'd already given up on himself. Maud eventually had Lee move in with him. She was too worried to leave your dad alone so she sent her husband to look after him."

"Greet never told me." More significant history she wasn't privy to.

"Senior year of high school I bought a little dingy with an outdoor motor." He smiled, remembering. "I think it ran for an entire week before the engine gave out. I took a chance and knocked on your dad's door. He opened it and saw my truck on the street with a boat in tow. Maybe I imagined it, but I think I saw his eyes light up. An hour later he had that motor purring like a kitten. Two hours and the both of us were off shore with our lines in the water."

"Why didn't he bring me back? As he got better, I would've thought he'd bring me home again." Annie held the truffle but her sweet tooth was lost.

"I don't know. I used to bring you up in conversation, but he'd shut down and wouldn't answer my questions. I do know I used to pray that you'd come home. That wasn't answered either."

"I'm sorry Menno, for everything about this story, for my dad and you and me. I've struggled with all of it. Dad was my best mate. We did everything together. I remember the first time he took me scuba diving. He helped me into this heavy equipment and put a tank on my back. I could hardly stand up with all of it on. He picked me up, gear and all, and carried me into the water. He asked me if I was afraid." She ran her finger around the rim of the mug. "I felt like I should be, everything being so strange, and what we were about to do. I told him 'no'. I was with my dad and he made life fun. We sank below the surface together and he held my hand as we circled the reef. So many fish. And all the colors, it was like I'd fallen into a magical world I never knew existed. There it was, right before me. My father had brought me to a fairy-tale land." She grinned. "For a while I thought it was something only my dad knew about. I couldn't believe he was hiding this underwater world from everyone else. Once we surfaced, I threw myself at him, my arms too small to hug him. I yelled, 'I did it! I breathed underwater!' He wrapped me in a hug and whispered, 'You did it baby girl. You can breathe underwater. It'll always be your superpower.'"

"You two had such a close relationship," Menno said. "I think I was always a little jealous of it."

"He used to let me tag along wherever he went. I remember being so proud of him. What exactly happened to my once happy father?"

"There's only one person who can explain any of this to you. You'll have to ask him."

Chapter Twelve

The sound of clinking coffee mugs and silverware being slid into bus bins broadcast throughout the Bon Air Café. The smell of freshly brewed coffee and crispy bacon filled the air. As Annie walked inside her morning immediately looked up. She searched and found Puck sitting at a booth under the front window. He was in his work clothes, blue pants and matching shirt. His neon yellow vest and hard hat were on the bench next to him. Despite it being early morning, the man appeared worn out.

"Good morning, Puck."

"Annie, thanks for meeting me before my shift." He stood as she took her seat. Corrie arrived carrying two mugs and a pot of coffee and placed them on the table.

"Thanks, Corrie," Puck said.

Corrie put her hand on her hip and looked down at Annie. "What's this all about?" She gestured between them. "Are you going to the dark side right here for everyone to see? Remember, Puck is the enemy."

"I'm sitting right here," he said. "I can hear everything you're saying."

"Good morning, Corrie." Annie put a splash of cream in her coffee. "Puck will never be the enemy, he's our friend. By the way, we intend to have a nice chat with minimal interruption if you get what I mean."

"Have it your way." She placed menus on the table and left them.

"She means well," Annie said. "She's just looking out for Greet."

"One thing Greet's not short on are friends. Boy, it took her a long while to get over losing you."

"You were there for her," Annie said. "We'd talk or text constantly the first few months I was in New York. She always told me what a huge support you were for her. I felt jealous. There I was on my own and she had you."

"Damn, I wish you were here when we found out she was pregnant with Nel." Puck swiped his palm down over his mouth and chin. "She really could've used some support. Don't get me wrong, her parents were great, jovial, almost. But it was a lot to go through at nineteen. Even before we got the news we were going to be parents, we used to talk about getting married. She had dreams of how our wedding would be. San Bernardo's Church and a pretty white dress. All of our family and friends. Afterward a reception at the harbor club. Lots of food and an open bar." He looked out the window. "In the end, it was just the two of us at the courthouse in front of a judge."

"Greet never once complained about the way you two were married."

"She's too good a person to whine. Truth is, I think that was just the beginning."

"Beginning? Of what?"

"More coffee?" Corrie picked up the pot and topped off their mugs. "Puck, don't you think you ought to skedaddle? Annie's here on vacation, she doesn't have time to listen to your confession. Give the girl a break."

"Corrie, really, we're fine." Annie smiled. "I actually do want to talk to my friend Puck. If you want to help, you can bring us two of the pirate pancake platters."

"Extra butter and maple syrup," Puck added.

"With a side of that delicious bacon I smell," Annie said.

"Now go skedaddle yourself," Puck said, "Or we'll stiff you on the tip."

"Fine." With an exaggerated eye roll, she left.

"The beginning of me being a huge disappointment," Puck whispered. "In the end, she was forced to marry me. Sure, we'd talked about it, but we thought it would be after we both graduated college. Not instead of college. I worked as much as I could trying to have a little extra spending money. It just never seemed like we had enough. And poor Greet, being on her feet all day at that salon."

"So, you left her because, you love her."

"Don't look at me like I'm crazy Annie Martis. We got in a huge argument about going back to school. We both want to take classes, but there's no way we could do it at the same time and pay the bills. She wants a better life than I can offer her. She's so beautiful and kind, and, and any guy would be lucky to have her. It would be easy for her to find someone who could provide her with a better life."

"You know you're crazy, right? She loves you and you've gone and broken her heart. She thinks you've got a girlfriend for crying out loud."

"What? No, never."

"And how exactly is leaving her helping?"

"After I left, Maud offered her a place to stay so she could go back to school. With me out of the picture, she can better herself, get a degree, find a man more worthy of her love."

"And what about sweet Nel?"

"I was wondering the same thing," Corrie said, placing two plates heaping full of pancakes and bacon in front of them. "I never pegged Puck for a deadbeat dad, but he's earned that label all on his own."

"Again, I'm sitting right here."

"Thanks, Corrie." Annie smiled at her friend and waited for her to take her leave.

"I love Nel more than life itself," he said, once the coast was clear. "I'll always be her dad."

"Good Lord, Puck." Annie poured syrup over the warm stack, the pad of butter melted and slid down the side. "I better eat up. I've got a lot of work to do."

Puck cut into his stack but moved the pancakes around the plate more than he ate them. Annie, finding a renewed appetite, finished the entire pile. Corrie removed the dishes and topped their mugs once more.

"I better get to work," Puck said. "It's so good to see you. Thanks for coming down to support Greet. She, and I, appreciate it more than you'll ever know." He stood and slid his arms into his vest and put his helmet in place. He pulled out his wallet.

"Breakfast is my treat," Annie said. "Since I invited you."

"Thanks, Annie."

"Puck," Corrie placed two platters in his hands. "Deliver these to table seven for me, will you?" She smiled at him then took his now empty seat at the booth. Puck shook his head and headed to the booth in the corner.

"He knows the table numbers?" Annie asked.

"Everyone knows them." A couple walked in the door. "Have a seat at eleven," Corrie yelled to them. "I'll be a few minutes, help yourselves to coffee."

"Taking a break?"

"I just want a little alone time with you before everyone grabs all your attention again."

"I'm sorry, Corrie. I didn't mean to—"

"I understand. I'm the only one not going through a crisis right now. The squeaky wheel always gets the grease." She leaned back in the booth. "It sure is good to have you home. Tell me, how does it feel being back? It must be so different from New York."

"They're two different worlds. Not to say one is better than the other. Both have pluses and minuses."

"What's the biggest plus in New York?"

"Oh, let me think." Her eyes lit up. "The food, the different cultures. I live within a ten minute walk of the most delicious dishes. The Thai restaurant serves som tam. It's a salad made with tamarind juice and fish sauce."

"If you say so."

"The Italian place on the corner puts parma ham on absolutely everything, melon, pizza, focaccia. Don't even get me started on the goi cuon at the Vietnamese diner. That establishment is now run by the family's fourth generation."

"Sounds amazing. What else?"

"Gosh, Corrie, the museums alone would take years to visit. We have some of the best art galleries. Enough on and off Broadway productions to sink a small ship. We've caught a Knick's game at the Garden each season for as long as I can remember."

"So much to do. You must never get bored."

"The pace and pulse of the city takes a little getting used to."

"How would someone make the move there? If they wanted to live in the city, what do you think the first steps should be?"

"You? You want to move away?"

"Shocking, isn't it?" Corrie said. "I look like I've got it all. I get to be a waitress at the Bon Air Café and live with my parents." She raised her arms. "What's not to love about all of this?"

"I had no idea you were unhappy here."

"Not completely but I am curious, and a bit restless. I have a four year degree in marketing and I'm still waiting tables. There aren't a lot of opportunities here for me. I loved studying consumer behavior, price strategies and managing competitor research." She sat up as another group came in. "I need to quit feeling sorry for myself and get back to work."

"I think you should give it a go, take a chance." Annie reached out to her. Corrie took her hands. "You happen to have a connection in Manhattan who would be glad to put you up while you interview and search for a job. I have a little downstairs apartment but there are extra bedrooms upstairs. I'm sure my aunt and uncle would love to host you. I can show you the city, it'll be fun."

"It will be, won't it?" She climbed out of the booth. "I'll be back soon."

"Where are you going?"

"I need to work on my resume. Cover these tables until I get back, will you?"

"Hi Orion," Annie said as she and Nel walked into the salon. She searched the shop and saw her friend. "Hey Greet. We're just stopping in to say hello on our way to the beach."

"Hi guys," Greet called from her station. "Looks like you've got a fun morning planned."

"Don't you two look like a couple of bathing beauties," Orion said.

Annie wore a terrycloth cover-up over her bathing suit and had borrowed a pair of Greet's flip flops. She carried a woven bag with colorful towels and a large hat spilling out the top. In her other hand was a cooler filled with sandwiches, snacks, and a thermos of cold tea. Nel had her purple suit on and wore plastic sunglasses that matched. An oversized inflatable flamingo gave her fits as she tried to steady the obtuse floatable.

"Aunt Annie's going to take me swimming," the young girl said. "She said I have to ride a horse again."

"You have to get back on the horse after you've fallen off," Annie corrected.

"I fell off a horse?" She squinted. "I don't remember it."

Annie and Greet worried that Nel would develop a fear of the water as a result of her accidental fall in the ocean. They agreed it would be a good idea to get her back swimming again as soon as possible.

"Nel," Annie said. "Will you take a seat in the waiting area while I talk to Orion? Maybe there's a magazine you'd like to look through."

"I'll check out the fashions." She hopped on a chair, feet sticking straight out in front of her, and found something to look through. Annie followed Orion to her usual workstation in front of the picture window.

"What can I do for you?" Orion asked as they sat across from each other. "Manicure?"

"Oh, no thank you, my nails still look great." She looked over her shoulder, assuring herself they wouldn't be overheard. "I'm on a sort of a mission."

"Do tell."

"I have to get Greet and Puck back together before I leave for home tomorrow." She dropped her voice. "I've spoken with them both individually. I know this sounds hard to believe, but they're still in love, just stubborn."

"Stubborn is a tough one," Orion said. "What's the plan?"

"That's where this gets tricky," Annie said. "I have no plan. I was kind of hoping you'd help me come up with one."

"Smart girl, coming to me. Let's see, how do we get two people, who are clearly in love with each other, back together?"

"Two stubborn people."

"Yes, very stubborn."

"This can't be that hard," Annie said. "We just need to be shrewd."

"Right, shrewd, and also a bit cagy. We don't want our meddling to get out." Orion looked around the salon. "What can we use to bring them together? Something they both have a strong connection to."

"They both love dancing and music," Annie offered. "At least, they used to."

"Aunt Annie I found a pink hat with feathers!" Nel called from across the room waving a magazine over her head. "I want one so bad!"

"Bingo," Orion said.

"We use Nel."

"Let's put our beach towels and cooler over here." Annie and Nel walked over the warm sand. The sky was the color of sweet forget-me-nots and the sun was still climbing, allowing for a temperate morning. Annie dug in the oversized bag and removed the sunscreen and towels. She tossed her coverup on the inflated flamingo and squeezed the cream onto their palms. They took turns getting each other's backs, and when they were both covered, headed toward the shoreline.

"No more swimming in my princess dress," Nel said. "I got my purple sparkle tank on."

"That suit was made for in the ocean," Annie said. "You'll do just fine today."

They held hands and advanced slowly, Annie discreetly gauging Nel's response to the water. They stopped when the swash ran up and covered their toes. "Oh, that feels nice and warm," Annie said. "Let's go in up to our knees."

"My knees or your knees?" Nel asked. "'Cause we'll hit mine first."

"Right you are smart-Alec. How about my knees?"

They inched in slowly, knees, hips then waist. The clear and calm water enticing them further. Suddenly, Nel pulled her hand from Annie's and dove under an approaching swell.

"Nel!" Annie called out, but the girl surfaced with a huge smile.

"Come on in Aunt Annie! It's fun! Get your stupid bun wet." And she sunk underneath again and swam toward her aunt. Popping up out of the water in front of her, she pulled her arm back then drove it over the surf, covering Annie in seawater.

"That's it," Annie laughed, "You're gonna get it now." She lunged at Nel and held her by the waist. The girl was too big to be lifted very high, but Annie made a good effort. She tossed Nel who squealed and giggled as she sunk below the surface again.

"And my bun isn't stupid." She thought a moment, considered her surroundings, and worked the elastic out of her hair. Shaking her locks free, she slid the band on her wrist and dove into the sea.

They chased each other through the water, practiced handstands in the shallows and floated on their backs with their eyes closed, soaking up the sunshine. Nel pointed out fish that were living in the clumps of coral around them. She didn't know the specific species names and simply labeled them, blue fish, yellow fish, and rainbow fish.

When their fingers turned to prunes, they trudged out and fixed their towels on the sand. Annie found her book in the beach bag and leaned back to read. Nel played in the sand, her imagination running, as seashells became mermaids and driftwood their homes. The sun inched to its peak and more families arrived on the beach.

"I don't know about you, but I'm hungry," Annie said, closing her book. "Ready for a sandwich?"

"I'm hungry just like you." Nel watched the people as they settled along the coast. "Hey, here comes Menno."

Annie straightened and searched the shoreline. There he was. Coming toward them in just his swim trunks, Annie had to take a breath and still her racing heart. Looking back, he was a funny looking kid. Teeth too big for his mouth and brown eyes that claimed too much space on his face. As a preteen, his features softened and in high school he easily turned heads. But this Menno had definitely grown into a real stunner.

Think of Stewart. Look away. Why am I staring? "Oh, Menno, yes, there he is." *Stop looking.* But it was too late, he'd seen her and waved. She threw her arm in the air and held it there. *What are you doing? Put your arm down.* She dropped her hand and stood as he approached.

"You picked the perfect day for the beach," Menno said. "Not too hot and the water's nice and calm."

"Aunt Annie doesn't have her bun. I told her it was stupid."

"I imagine she found it practical," he said. "But she sure looks like a new person without it." He grinned at Annie. "I don't want to interrupt—"

"No, not at all," Annie said. "We were just about to eat lunch. I'd be glad to share if you'd like to join us." *What am I doing? I'm engaged to be married. Think of Stewart.*

"I'd love that, thanks."

"I can sit on my flamingo if you want to use my towel," Nel said, pulling the bouncy bird closer to the cooler.

Once all situated, Annie popped the lid off a sandwich keeper and passed it to Menno. He chose a half and handed it to Nel who fished out a peanut butter and jelly. Annie unscrewed the thermos and filled two cups with iced tea. She filled the lid for herself. From the beach bag, she pulled some chips and with a little effort managed to open them. The other half of the turkey and cheese had her name on it and she scooped it up.

"This is nice, thanks for the invitation," Menno said, taking a bite. He grabbed a handful of salt and vinegar.

"Not working today?" Annie buried her feet in the sand.

"No, I give myself two days off a week. If I didn't plan it, I'd be there all the time. This afternoon a group of us are getting together to set up the festival of lights."

"Oh? I don't remember such a thing." Annie took a bite and washed it down.

"It was Father O'Brian's idea a few years back. We create a tunnel of holiday lights that runs from the elementary school to the town square. Families gather at the school on Christmas Eve and Santa invites them to follow him to the North Pole. A line a mile long walks into the red, green, and white passageway. We place some fun lit characters along the way. The church choir walks with the group leading everyone in carols."

Annie was covered with goosebumps just hearing the description. She dug into the bag of chips and pulled out a handful. A few fell to the sand and instantly attracted a seagull.

"It really is something," he said. "As everyone approaches the town square, Santa takes his throne and begins passing gifts to all the children."

"I bet the kids love that."

"Last year, the women's auxiliary sponsored a *Little Miss Snowflake* contest. We set up a small stage and the kids that entered had to tell the crowd what Christmas meant to them. It was really cute. There's a toddler division, right up to seniors in high school."

"Sounds absolutely adorable. I'm sorry I'm going to miss it."

"Done!" Nel jumped up. "Can I go back in?"

"You only ate half your sandwich," Annie said. "I made that peanut butter and jelly at your request."

Nel rolled her eyes and took a bite of the remaining half.

"Don't you want some chips?"

She took a few and chomped them quickly. "Done again."

"Okay silly. You can go back in."

She dragged the bright flamingo across the sand. After maneuvering it out into waist deep water, they watched as she tried several times to climb on. As her attempts failed, she fell head over heels into the water only to try again. Her giggles traveled over the surface and back to Annie and Menno.

"After what happened the other day Greet and I were worried she might be afraid of the water."

"No need to be concerned about that," Menno said as they watched Nel splash about. "She's been in the water since before she could walk. As an infant, Greet and Puck used to put her in a contraption that kept her afloat. It wasn't long until she wanted to be in the water with them."

They finished lunch and Annie put the containers back in the cooler. She looked up and gaged the position of the sun. "I'm going to catch some rays while I can. It's bound to be snowing in New York when I get back." She positioned her towel and found the sunscreen. "I better apply some more. This northern skin won't know what hit it."

"I think I'll join Nel," he said. "Maybe give her a hand with that flamingo."

Annie watched as he splashed into the surf to the delight of the little girl. Before long she was diving off his shoulders and being thrown properly into the air. After applying the lotion, she laid back and closed her eyes.

"Annie you better cover up." Greet was standing over her. "I'm taking Nel home with me, she's a prune. Thanks for taking her today."

"What time is it?" Annie sat up confused. "I must've fallen asleep." Families had left the beach and the onshore breeze had a nip to it. "Where's Nel?"

"I'm right here." Nel stood wrapped in her towel.

"We thought we'd let you rest," Menno said. "Greet just got here."

"I should go with you." Annie stood, still a bit out of it. "I could use a shower and I should text Stewart. Menno, thanks for staying and watching Nel."

"It was fun."

"I forgot how pretty your hair is," Greet said. "You should wear it down more often. We'll see you back at the house." She ushered Nel along.

"Okay, I'll be right behind you," Annie called after them.

"Now that you're well rested, how about dinner tonight?" Menno said. "You and me, what do you say?"

"Sounds a little like a date."

"That's because it definitely is a date."

"But I'm—"

"I know, engaged, but you're not married yet. One date Annie, for old time's sake."

"I guess—"

"Great, I'll pick you up at seven."

Chapter Thirteen

"Greet!" Annie yelled down the stairs. Her hair was dripping and she stood in her bra and panties. She held a bath towel in front of herself. "Can I— may I invade your closet again?" She had looked through everything she brought, straight legged slacks and heavy linen dresses more suitable for the office than the island. Not one thing appropriate for a date. More importantly, nothing that she'd want Menno to see her in.

"Sure." Greet appeared at the bottom of the stairs. "Why don't I help you look. It'll be fun." She trotted up the steps and into her room. "You sit on the bed and I'll pull some things for you to try." She pushed open the doors and walked inside. "Any idea where he's taking you?"

"No, but he said it was a real date."

"This is Menno, that could mean anything." She found her cell and touched the screen. "Hey, it's me. Throw me a bone, will you? We're trying to decide what to wear." She listened for a second. "Got it. Thanks." She touched End. "Okay, so you were right, this is an actual date." She slid hangers down the bar, studying her wardrobe as she went. She pulled a flowered print dress with a wide ribbon around the waist. "This one's cute. I wore it to a baby shower last spring."

Annie considered the outfit. "No, too churchy."

After looking again Greet produced a flowing orange one with a V-neck. "How about this. Super comfortable."

Annie squished her face. "I look horrible in that color."

"Okay." She went back to work and found a black midi with a capped sleeve.

"Too business casual."

"How about this one." It had a full skirt and small ruffle.

"Pink? I'll look like Nel."

Greet studied it. "You're right about that. Okay, agreed, no pink." She rehung it and searched some more. "What would I wear on a date with Menno?" She stopped and looked at her friend. "Tell me something. Are we trying to impress him or drive him off? Because I can see you going either way."

"Well," she quieted. "I should be driving him off, but—"

"But it's Menno. Your first love." Greet sat on the bed and took Annie's hand.

"Yes, it's Menno." She laid her head on Greet's shoulder. "What am I doing? I'm engaged to Stewart. My home is in New York." She whispered, "But it's—"

"I think I have the perfect dress." Greet went back into the closet. "Let me help you put this one on."

Annie stood in front of the full length mirror. Greet was behind her, both looking at the image reflected. The pale green fabric was covered in tiny, embroidered flowers and stopped just above her knee. Her hair flowed freely past her shoulders and down her back.

"Menno's going to fall down when he sees this sweetheart neck-line," Greet said. The sun had Annie glowing and her chest was just a tease at the edge of the fabric.

"This dress is beautiful," Annie said. She touched her hair and ran a finger over her tanned cheek. "I look like me again." She turned and hugged her friend. "Thank you."

They chose a pair of sling backs and added a necklace. When they went downstairs, Annie was surprised to see both Maud and Orion there.

"Sorry Annie," Greet said. "News travels like a freight train in this town."

"We just wanted to see you off," Maud said. "Annie, you look beautiful."

"It's like prom night all over again," Orion said. "Greet, you and Annie stand in front of the tree. I want to snap some photos."

They giggled like school girls as they stood for the pictures. Nel jumped in and then they all took turns joining in and then taking the pictures, until they had every possible combination covered. While Annie was posed between Maud and Orion, their hands resting on her shoulders, she could only think of the mother that was missing from this one. The lost soul was somewhere in the air, as all three had to dab their cheeks and fight the tears. The picture taking was interrupted by a knock on the door. They waited, knowing Menno would let himself in. When the door didn't open, Annie went to answer it.

"Menno, they're beautiful." He handed her a colorful bouquet. "So thoughtful, thank you." She held them to her nose. The unmistakable scent of spring, here in the middle of December.

"Not nearly as pretty as you." He noticed her dress. "Wow. You look— perfect."

"Please, come in." After that reaction to the dress, she caught Greet's eye and winked. "Maud and Orion stopped by. I'm sure they'd like to say hello."

"Hi Menno," Maud said. "So nice to see you. We were just taking some pictures. How about one of you and Annie?"

"Maud," Orion said. "This isn't prom night. They're two adults going out on a date."

"Exactly," Maud replied. "Just like their junior prom."

They obediently stood in front of the fire as Maud captured several images. Menno wore jeans, a crisp white collared shirt, and a navy sport jacket. He seemed to blush and Annie's expression turned shy when they were asked to stand closer together. When Maud was pleased, she took the flowers from Annie and promised to put them in water.

"But before I do," Maud said, pulling a single stem from the bundle and snapping it short, "This will look lovely tucked behind your ear." She slid a pink mum into Annie's hair and used a bobby pin to secure it.

"Thanks Maud," Annie said, touching the delicate flower. She was wearing pink tonight, like it or not.

"Shall we go?" Menno gestured toward the door and with well wishes from their friends, walked outside. He opened the passenger door of his truck and Annie climbed in.

"Thank you," he said while pulling away from the curb.

"For what?"

"Going out with me tonight." He grinned and shot a glance at her legs. "And for that dress."

Annie was surprised when they arrived at the new hotel in town. Large wreaths with red bows hung on the main doors. Menno pulled one open and they went inside. They entered into the lobby and were immediately drawn to a massive Christmas tree displayed in the center of the rotunda. It was decorated with ocean themed bobbles created from fine glass. Octopus, angelfish, and lobsters reflected the tiny white lights that encircled the tree. Packages wrapped in blue and green paper were tucked underneath. Instrumental carols played quietly in the background. He touched her shoulder and pointed skyward. The area was open to the floors above. Garlands of green and white lights circled the balconies above, beyond them, the ceiling twinkled like the night sky.

He took her hand and led her toward the hostess stand. He gave his name and they followed the woman to a table in the restaurant. The lighting was soft and the decorations spectacular. The entire ceiling was covered in gold, red and green balls. Interspersed were sprigs of evergreen. The almost imperceptible scent of pine drifted around them. They were seated near a fireplace large enough to stand in. The mantel held more candles than Annie could count. White, red, gold, and green, the flickering tapered flames a romantic addition to the already dreamy room.

Menno pulled back her chair. Annie slid her hand over her bottom, tucking her dress underneath, as she sat. He took his seat and they both placed the crisp linen napkins on their laps. On the table, a hurricane lamp glimmered from a ring of red berries. A man arrived and filled their water glasses from a silver pitcher. A second man approached and handed them menus.

"Good evening and welcome," the server said. He explained how the duck and the salmon were prepared and described the filet they were offering. "I'll give you a minute to peruse the dinner options. May I bring you something to drink?"

"I was thinking a sparkling wine would be nice." He looked at Annie. "Should we order the Prosecco?"

"Yes, thank you, that sounds delicious."

They were fussed over and treated like royalty by the staff. Their flutes refilled as soon as they were empty and dishes whisked away after each course. They shared oysters on the half shell as an appetizer and struggled with their dinner decisions. In the end Menno ordered the filet mignon, rare with garlic potatoes, and Annie the pan seared sea bass with lemon butter.

Annie stole glimpses of her date as he enjoyed his meal. The candlelight flickered over his strong jaw and sharp nose and twinkled in his dark eyes. He had planned a wonderful evening. Something occurred to Annie.

"May I ask a prying question?"

"Of course," he said. "Pry away."

"How is it that you're still single?" She gestured at their surroundings. "You really know how to impress a woman. I imagine available ladies would find you a great catch."

"I haven't been single all this time." He put down his fork. "I've never married, but I have dated on and off. There was one woman who I saw as a lifetime partner. We were together over almost two years and I thought we'd eventually be married."

"What happened?"

"She worked in information technology. I thought she had the best of both worlds. She could make a good living working from home."

"Sounds ideal."

"We were together over a year when she started making comments about the island being so small." He picked up his fork but only dragged it through the potatoes. "I've always thought that was a positive, the island is like a home. Everything we need is right here. She didn't see it that way. She took a job in Amsterdam and that was the end of us."

"I'm sorry."

"I know living here can be a hardship for some. We don't always have the luxuries available to people living on a mainland. Our supplies arrive by plane and boat and aren't always on schedule. Not everyone is willing to live this way."

"In New York we seldom lack for anything." She lifted her wine and looked into the rising bubbles. "I remember growing impatient when a ball point pen I ordered wasn't on my desk the following day. I'd paid extra for express shipping." She shook her head. "The pen was coming from Paris." Sheepishly, she added, "I've become a bit of a snob."

"Maybe, but you seem to be recovering." He smiled.

"It's a different world there. The noises, the hustle and bustle. There's just a certain energy you can actually feel in the air when you walk down the streets."

"I know, it's crazy." He cut into his steak.

"You know?" Her eyebrows dropped. "What do you mean, you know?" His face went flush as he put his utensils on his plate. She could feel her heart speed up. "When have you ever been to New York?" He remained silent, studying his dinner. "Menno, please. When did you visit New York?"

"I toured Columbia University."

"What?" She fell back in her chair. "You told me you thought about transferring. You never said you visited the campus."

"I came to New York hoping to eventually move there and be with you again. They accepted me for their fall semester. This all happened while you were refusing my calls. I'm guessing you blocked my number because I would never get a response from you."

"I did. I was trying to forget you." She stared, hardly believing what she was hearing.

"After touring the campus, I knocked on the brownstone's door. Your aunt answered. She went quite pale when she realized who I was. I can't blame her. I gave her an awful time after your mom's funeral. When I realized she was taking you, I said some horrible things to her and your uncle. She did invite me in, although reluctantly."

"You were at the brownstone? How is it I was never told any of this?"

"Your aunt was very nice. If I remember correctly, she offered me a cola. We sat in the front room, the one with the fireplace, and talked for a while." He grinned, but it wasn't a happy one. "I was so excited to share my news with you but you weren't in. Peggy explained to me that you'd finally settled in and New York was your home. It had taken you over a year, but she thought you were happy. She suggested it would be a bad idea to disrupt your life at such a critical time. I guess you were dating a guy named, Harrison, or was it Charleston? I can't recall, but she thought he was the one."

"The one? I don't even remember the guy's name. Donovan, maybe. I think we went out once or twice."

"I had a flight home that afternoon. I couldn't afford to stay more than a day. The hotel rooms were quite expensive. When I got back to Bonaire, I started adding up costs. They'd offered me a sweet scholarship so tuition and room and board weren't a concern. But the travel back and forth would add up. That, and the possibility you were no longer interested, made me rethink the entire idea. I tried calling you several more times and when I never got a reply, well, that was the end of that."

A server appeared and cleared the dinner plates. A haunting rendition of *What Child is This* hung in the air and the two had little to say. Menno paid the bill, stood, and held Annie's chair as she rose. They walked through the dining room and as they reached the hostess stand, Annie took his hand in hers. For all the times in her life she had let herself dream of what could have been, she never realized how close her fantasy once was to becoming a reality. She had cut him off and in turn, severed every possibility for their future together. They stopped at the gorgeous tree for one last look, neither saying a word, then left the hotel.

"I shouldn't have told you." Menno broke the silence when they were back in his truck and heading toward town. "I didn't mean to ruin our date, I'm sorry."

"Please, don't be sorry. I feel like I've been stabbed in my heart all over again, but still, I'm glad I know. We might have been together all this time if it weren't for my stupid actions. Maybe you would've fallen in love with Manhattan and we'd be living and working there together."

"Or," he offered. "We could've earned our degrees and then moved back to Bonaire."

"Why would we do that? What good is an education in high finance if you can't work on Wall Street?" Her thoughts ran wild. "If I had been home the day you came to the brownstone, I probably would've taken one look at you and the two of us would've high tailed it back to the island, no degrees at all."

"Or maybe we would've crashed and burned like a lot of couples."

"No, don't say that. In another time, in another life, you and me, we would've worked out. I'm sure of it."

"I think you're right." He put his hand on hers. "Now you're a big shot in love with another big shot."

"Yes, and Stewart and I work well together, we're a good match."

"But look at Greet and Puck. No one saw that coming, and now they've split up."

"Don't bet your money on it. Orion and I are working on a plan to get them back together."

"I like the sound of that. Let me know if I can help." He pulled into a parking area and turned off the engine. "If you're up for it, I thought we'd stop in The Drunken Mermaid for a nightcap."

As they entered the dark room, they were bombarded with laughter and lively chatter from the throng of patrons. Just inside the door, a life-sized wooden mermaid sat on the end of the bar with a shot glass in her hand. She wore two seashells as a top and her delicately carved tail fin fell over the edge. Someone had put a Santa hat on her head.

Menno grabbed the bartender's attention and ordered two draft beers. He handed one to Annie. "I trust you'll still like the local stuff."

She didn't consider herself a beer drinker but the thick head and cool brew had her rethinking that. After a substantial taste, she wiped the foam from her upper lip and caught her breath.

"That is really good," she said.

A band was setting up out back. Menno took her hand and led her through the crowd. The one story building was open to the outside and the ocean crashed on the shore just a few yards away. The sky was clear and filled with stars, a slight breeze cooled them. As the guitarist strummed a few notes the crowd began to trickle onto the back patio.

Menno found a seat near the water. They watched as the band found it's rhythm and dancers took to the floor. It wasn't long until they'd formed a line and began moving together.

"Care to dance?" Menno asked.

"I'm afraid I've never line danced." She was drawn to the enthusiastic dancers as the lines moved in perfect unison. "It does look fun, though."

"Come with me, it's easy." He took her hand and they stood watching the moves. "See, it's only six or seven steps, then a turn, and repeat."

Once Annie saw the pattern and thought she had it down, they joined in. Three steps to the right, tap, grapevine to the left, two steps back, tap, step front, slide back, scuff the heal, and turn.

"You got this!" Menno laughed next to her. "Look at you, you're a natural!"

The song ended and some people left the floor. The band segued to a nostalgic jazz number and Menno took Annie's hand.

"Now I know you can swing with the best of them."

Annie beamed as her feet pranced over the floor. She miraculously remembered the moves she hadn't danced since she was a teen. With Menno leading her, it all came back. Soon he had her twirling under his arm and being propelled backward and then snatched up close again.

The singer yelled over the dancers, "What will Santa Claus say when he arrives and finds everybody swinging?"

As Menno caught her in his arms over and again, she could hardly believe she was here. Dancing on Bonaire with the man she once loved. The man whom at one time was her everything. As the song morphed to a slow tune, he held her close, palm in the small of her back, and swept her over the floor with ease.

"Annie Martis?" A surprised voice next to them. "No way."

"Dewey?" Annie's eyes were wide. "I can't believe it."

"I haven't seen you since we sunk my dad's dinghy in the lake." He looked at Menno. "Sorry buddy, I'm cutting in."

Menno gave a salute and half bowed as he backed away. Annie danced with her old friend. They caught up, as well as they could, amidst the music and activity. Dewey waved over another one of Annie's childhood chums and she danced and laughed with him. His wife saw Annie and cut in, insisting she needed to hug and welcome her friend home. When the band announced they were taking a break, the crowd clapped and whistled and Annie returned to the table. She had worked up a thirst and turned her beer up, finishing the entire thing.

"That was quite a workout," she huffed.

"I'm glad you've gotten to see some of the old gang." Menno grinned but Annie saw the sadness in it. "I have to say something before it's too late." He took her hand. "I can't let you leave the island without you knowing how I feel. I love you, Annie. I always have."

"Menno—"

"There's never been anyone else like you. Don't you feel it? There's something between us that was never fully lost. I feel it still, love, I love you, Annie Martis."

"Menno—"

"Say it Annie, I know it's in your heart. Tell me you love me."

"I don't know how to use that word."

"We used to say it all the time," he said. "It comes naturally for us, try Annie, say you love me and make it so."

"I can't do it. I can't use that word, I'm sorry."

The silence was deafening and the short drive home covered a million miles. After parking in front of Greet's house, he circled to Annie's side. He walked her to the door and took her hand.

"Get a good night's rest," he said. "I'm picking you up at eight."

"Menno, I don't think that's a good—"

"Be ready to go." He started toward his truck and called over his shoulder, "And wear a swimsuit."

Chapter Fourteen

Like an excited child on Christmas morning, Annie woke well before her alarm. The anticipation of spending the morning with Menno had her feeling a little giddy. She made herself stay in bed until the first morning light began to creep into her room. With it, came the promise of a beautiful day. The house was quiet. After brushing her teeth and a washcloth to her face, she found her swimsuit and cover-up. In the kitchen she scribbled a quick note letting Greet know she was with Menno. The clock read 7:55 a.m. She placed the paper near the coffeemaker and, at the front door, slid her feet into Greet's flipflops. The door closed behind her with a gentle click.

"Right on time." Menno stood by his truck.

"I couldn't sleep." She smiled. "I have a sneaking suspicion of what you have planned for us this morning." She stood on her tiptoes and peered into the vehicle's bed. "Yes!"

"I thought, for old time's sake," he said, "we'd go down to the salt pier and see what we can find."

Annie took a closer look. Air cylinders and scuba diving equipment filled the bed. Masks, fins, and snorkels, along with the inflatable vests, breathing regulators and mouthpieces. Everything they would need to explore the ocean's depths.

She lifted a piece of gear and studied it. Her face dropped as she stared at the pink fin. "You kept my diving gear." She glanced at him and then lifted a mask, turning it in her hand. "It's all here, I can't believe it."

"Like seeing an old friend, isn't it?" he said. "I can't take all the credit. Your dad always had it at his place, I just stopped by and picked it up. He's been taking care of it all this time."

"My dad?"

"Every year or so he takes the regulator and vest to the dive shop to be serviced. Then, he puts it all away again. I can't be sure, but I think he's been hoping for the day you'll come home and need it."

"Did you tell him I was here?" She put the pieces back in the truck. "When you went to get my gear, does he know I'm on Bonaire?"

"It's a small island. He's known since the day you arrived."

"It's been so long." She gazed at the pile of hoses. "I hope I remember how to put it all together."

"Scuba is like riding a bike. You'll be fine." He opened the passenger side door and she hopped in. "By that grin on your face, I think I really nailed our second date."

"I'm so excited," she said, fastening her seatbelt. "I don't even care what you call it."

They drove south along the western shoreline, theirs was the only vehicle on the road. After a quiet ride, the pink salt beds appeared on their left. The site of them reminded Annie that Bonaire island produces some of the purest salts in the world. The sea water is harvested and left to evaporate in the sun, leaving rows of bright pink pools. Across the street, she saw the most vibrant turquoise water. Combined with the deep blue sky and a few puffy clouds, it was all what a picture postcard was made of. Annie felt a sort of calm as they approached.

Menno slowed the truck as they arrived at the pier. The massive structure was used to load pyramids of crystal white salt onto ships that would transport it around the globe. The area was currently free of any vessels and safe to dive. They bounced over the coral as he pulled into the site. He parked facing the water and they sat gazing at the spectacular ocean in front of them.

"I know he'd love to see you," Menno said.

"Are you sure? Because I don't know if I can stand to be rejected by him a second time."

"At the time," he turned in the seat to face her, "yes, that's what we both thought. We were young and could only see things through our own eyes. We saw your dad giving you away. Both of us believed that was what he was doing."

"It sure felt that way."

"He loved you Annie, he still does. He was destroyed by your mother's passing. At the time, he simply didn't have the capacity to care for you."

"You're saying he sent me to New York because he loved me?"

"Yes, that, and because he wanted the best for you. We couldn't understand it back then, we were only concerned about ourselves. But looking back, I realize what was going on. He'd fallen into a deep depression and had no medical help to get himself out of it."

"Thank you."

"For what?"

"Helping me to see it through your eyes."

"So, you'll go see him?"

"Maybe my next visit."

"I understand." His disappointment was visible. "Just promise me you'll take some time to think about it. I'd be happy to go along with you if that would make it easier."

"Speaking of making it easy." She got out of the truck, pulled her cover-up off and tossed it on the passenger seat. "How about helping me with this mishmash of equipment?"

Menno dropped the tailgate and they climbed into the bed. He moved the heavy air cylinders to the hatchback while Annie sorted through the other gear, placing hers together and organizing his in a separate pile. She was amazed to find it all came back to her. Remembering to be swift as to avoid getting her fingers pinched, she clamped the air to the back of her vest. Then she lifted her regulator and let the hoses fall freely. Studying it, she could picture where each one attached.

"How much weight do you want to carry?" Menno slid lead weights into the pockets of his vest. People were naturally buoyant. By carrying the heavy blocks, they would be able to sink and rise as they desired.

"I'll take eight pounds. There's no telling how dusty my buoyancy will be."

"No worries," he said, handing her the weight. "If it sinks you," he teased, "I'll pick you up off the bottom."

With the apparatus balancing at the edge of the lift, Annie only needed to slip her arms into the vest. She leaned forward, moving the heavy tank onto her back as she attached her Velcro belt and snaps. With mask, fins, and snorkel in hand, they moved carefully over the coral beach toward the water.

"I'm so excited!" Annie said. "It's been way too long."

"Scuba diving was your favorite activity. I'm a little shocked you didn't keep up with it. Isn't New York literally a coastal state? You've got beaches and islands there."

"Life changed."

Water swelled over her feet, a predictable eighty two degrees. The scattered clouds were giving way revealing a clear blue sky. She pushed a button and air flowed into her vest. Shuffling over the slippery corals, she eased herself in deeper. "I've forgotten how crystal clear this water is. Look there," she pointed, "Yellowtail snappers." A school of no fewer than twenty fish milled about just under the surface. Bright yellow tails grew from the pure white bodies. The golden stripe that ran from eye to tail made them easy to spy. "That's one fish I can actually remember."

"I bet there'll be a lot more."

When she was chest deep, she floated and struggled to pull on her fins. The waves didn't help as they pushed and pulled her about. Her feet flailed around as she tried to secure them. Once she won the battle, she tightened the straps behind her heels. Putting her mask on, she adjusted it to sit comfortably on her face.

"I'll feel better if I check your set-up." Menno moved around her, examining the connections running from air supply to her mouth, and to the vest itself. He checked the knob at the top of her cylinder. "Your tank is fully on. Everything looks right, you're good to go." He easily slid his feet into his fins and donned his mask. The current had moved them closer to the pier. "Let's descend here then swim underneath the structure. The pilings are always covered in life."

They placed their mouthpieces in and together disappeared below the surface. Once they had descended thirty feet, they adjusted the amount of air in their vests. With just the right amount, perfect buoyancy allowed them to float weightlessly through the calm water. The Caribbean ocean was so clear that Annie could easily see all her surroundings. Menno motioned for her to follow him. With just a few gentle kicks, they came upon a row of massive pilings that held up the huge structure above them. Barnacles, muscles, and crabs made their homes on the wooden beams. Several species of fish were finding an easy meal there. They swam between the pilings and headed out to depth. The only sound was their bubbles escaping and floating upward.

They advanced at a slow and pleasurable pace. A huge school of blue tangs churned up the water near them. The fish dove into the coral finding plankton and algae with their sharp teeth. The juveniles were still in their bright yellow stage and could be spotted swimming among the adults.

Menno pointed to the far end of the pier and Annie gave him the *okay* sign. Small baitfish were attracted to the food particles that wafted from the piling. They in turn attracted the larger fish. Annie wasn't surprised to see an individual barracuda hovering in the depths. It's formidable looking teeth had always kept Annie at a distance. She couldn't remember ever being afraid of ocean life, but the long and narrow fish could move through the water like an arrow and she was fine giving them space.

In a protected area created by the pilings, Annie saw an elusive queen angelfish. Its scales glowed like a neon sign under the sunbeams that cut through the surface. Truly a unique artwork of nature, it's yellow tail and blue body shimmered under the light. Annie floated closer and could see the queen's crown sitting neatly in place at the top of its head. She was falling behind and gave a few strong kicks and easily caught back up to Menno.

He pointed toward the open ocean. Sure enough, a cute pufferfish was advancing toward them. Its tubby body, large cow-like eyes and surprising grin made it a favorite of many divers. They swam side by side, advancing slowly. The familiar feel of her gear, the salty taste of the water and the calm that came with the quiet, all had Annie feeling a bit overwhelmed. This underwater world had once been a haven to her. From a young age, her father would take her diving and teach her the names of the fish, coral, and sponges. Even with the passage of time, this was one place she didn't feel like a stranger. She felt as though she were finally, truly, home.

Menno tapped her shoulder and pointed into the coral below them. She tried to find what he was drawing her attention to, but she didn't see anything unusual on the reef. He descended until he was able to point directly at a particular area. Still, she shook her head at him. He held up his index finger, indicating she should wait. As she stared at the spot, it glimmered.

The octopus, having been found, flashed burnt orange, darted just a few feet away, and camouflaged itself again. This time the divers had their eyes on it. They watched as the clever cephalopod changed its colors and perfectly blended into its new surroundings. They were just able to make out the eyes. They could see the siphon that moved water and enabled the animal to breathe.

They hovered calmly and soon the octopus went about its way. Its eight legs pulled the liquid like creature over the coral, perhaps looking for food. Finding none, it propelled itself along and was soon out of sight.

Annie clapped her hands and Menno gave her the thumbs up, both excited to have stumbled upon the incredible creature. They came to the end of the pier and she followed him to the right. More pilings were teaming with brightly colored fish. A grey angel seemed to want to tag along with them. A little white fish, just six inches or so, began swimming under Annie's belly. It had found a protected area there. She could see it as it darted out, grabbed a bite to eat, then dashed back underneath her.

Menno took her hand and motioned to go with him *this way*. He turned them westerly, out beyond the pier, and then simply let the current move them along. There, they saw an endless line of blue chromis swimming to the north. The small, yet brilliantly colored blue fish, were most likely heading to their feeding ground. The seemingly never-ending line shimmered in the sunlight, and made Annie think of the bright lights of Times Square.

Menno pointed at his dive computer and motioned back to shore. Time underwater was always limited due to the air supply getting low. As Annie turned toward shore, she felt tears pooling. This dive had been a true gift, one that magically took her back to some of the happiest moments of her young life.

They surfaced and floated about. They removed their masks and pushed dripping hair off their faces.

"Thank you for that," Annie said. "I'm just now realizing how much I've missed diving."

"I thought you'd like to put on your gear and get your feet wet. I'm glad you stayed long enough to work it in."

Annie heard a distant rumbling and squinted into the brightness above. A sleek 737 was cutting a white line across the sky. It was definitely the 10:20 flight on its way to Atlanta. Annie knew without a doubt it had at least one vacant seat onboard.

"Damn, I forgot about my flight."

They climbed out of the water, removed and disassembled the gear, and packed it all in the truck bed.

"What a beautiful day," Annie said, looking out at the water. "I'm not in a big hurry to leave. Do you have time for a swim?"

"I've cleared my calendar. I'm all yours." He shut the tailgate. "A swim sounds great. Do you see the buoy out there, floating at about one o'clock?"

"One o'clock?" She put her arm across her forehead, blocking the sun, and scanned the surface. "There it is, yes, I see it."

"I'll race you to it," he yelled as he took off toward the water.

"Cheater!" Annie called after him. "Whatever happened to one, two, three, go?" She dashed over the beach in an attempt to catch up.

They splashed into the water, Menno easily in the lead. At one time Annie would have given him a full head start and not even worry about catching up. She would always pass him and be the first one to the finish line. But it had been a long time since she raced across the ocean surface. At waist deep, she dove in and began an easy free-style stroke. Menno was out ahead. Every third stroke she peered up, checking her position. Her heart pounded and her leg muscles began to tire. She was out of breath when she stopped and treaded water.

Menno, having reached the buoy, saw Annie several yards away. He dug in and was next to her in no time.

"Are you okay?"

"Yes, I'm fine. Just out of shape." She laid her head back and floated. "I just need to catch my breath."

"If you're sure you're okay, I'd like to tell you something."

"What's that?" she huffed.

"I won."

They both laughed and Annie swiped a sheet of water at him. They did a lazy back stroke to shore, letting the sun warm them as they glided through the water. Menno filled her in on the where-abouts of her old high school friends. Several had left Bonaire, but more than half remained on the island. Many found work in the tourist industry.

When the sun was straight overhead, they left the water and drove to Menno's place. Annie sat at the table scratching Ginger behind her ears. Menno opened cabinets and searched through the refrigerator.

"May I lend a hand?" Annie asked.

"That would be great. I think I have everything to throw together a seafood salad. How are your chopping skills?"

"Sharp as a tack." Annie washed her hands then joined him at the counter. He placed a large wooden chopping board and knife in front of her.

"One stalk of finely sliced celery and a quarter cup of diced red onion." He put the vegetables on the board and removed shrimp and crab from containers.

"You've filled me in on the whereabouts and comings and goings our old friends," she said. "What about you?"

"What would you like to know?"

"Dad's General Store. How did you end up the owner?"

"Just by chance, really. After high school, I started working part time there. During college, the owner was happy to employ me over breaks and summer vacation. When he decided to retire to The Netherlands, he sold the shop to me at a reasonable fee."

"It was almost too easy," he continued. "I had my parents on standby in case things went south. But the shop continued to turn a profit. When the insurance agency next door went out of business, I bought that lot and expanded." He took the chopping board and knife and slid the ingredients into a bowl. "I just need to mix this all together. Grab some bread, will you?" He assembled the sandwiches then poured them each an iced tea.

They took their lunch to the front porch and Ginger trotted along behind them. Annie was surprised by her appetite. All the morning activities had her digging in. She held the overfilled hoagie in both hands and took a large bite.

"This is delicious," she said, mouth full. "Thank you."

"Thanks go to you for coming out with me today. After my inappropriate declaration last night. I owe you an apology."

"Last night? Don't worry, I've already put it aside." She took a second bite.

"I'm not sorry for what I said. I do love you. I'm only sorry the timing was wrong. For a minute there I thought I'd scared you away."

"I'm not that easy to scare." She put her sandwich on the plate. "I sound like a broken record, but I'm engaged to Stewart. I'm getting married this spring. My life is in New York now."

"But you belong—"

"I'm afraid what you're feeling are memories from the past. Even today. We dived and splashed in the ocean like a couple of kids. That's not real. We're not children anymore."

"You're wrong. Just because your job is your life doesn't mean that the rest of us stopped playing. Diving, swimming, swing dancing. It's a good life and not restricted to kids."

"I see your point, but you've got to understand. I simply don't have the time to play anymore."

Chapter Fifteen

"I think this will work." Annie said to Orion as she sat with her fingernails under the drying lamp. "If everything falls into place, and we get the reactions we need, we'll have Greet and Puck back together by this evening."

"I have a really good feeling about this," Orion said as she tidied her work space.

Greet stood at her station just yards away. Her scissors snipping and flying over a client's head. She shifted uncomfortably from foot to foot, clearly exhausted from all her stress and worry. Her face was pale and she was growing thin. Nel sat in a chair by the door waiting for her aunt to be finished.

"Nel, baby doll, come sit with me." Orion pulled a pad of paper and pencil from her drawer. "Sweetheart, we need you to write a few notes. Will you do that for us?"

Snowball Charlie joined Nel and Annie as they walked through town. Annie wanted to pick up some gifts to leave under Greet's tree.

After finding some pretty things for Maud and Orion, she made a stop in the stationary store to pick up something for Greet. There was no getting around the blizzard and two feet of snow that now blanketed the town square. Cars were directed around the icy blocks and the sidewalks now needed to be shoveled for shoppers. Annie tried to pick up the pace as they walked in front of *Dad's General Store*, but Nel and Charlie had to have a look in the window. They squished their noses up to the glass and cupped their faces in their hands. Menno had filled the display with an enchanting Christmas scene. A light covered tree with a billowy red skirt had attracted Ginger who slept in a ball on the soft fabric. Toys and puzzles, games and books filled the area.

"I'm going to ask Santa for one of those hover balls," Charlie said.

"I'm asking for that disco dance mat," Nel chimed in. "It plays music and has flashing lights. So cool."

"I'll share my gifts if you'll share yours."

"Sure," Nel said. "But my best gift is from Annie and Orion. They're getting my dad to come back home."

"Nel," Annie knelt in the snow and placed her palms on the girl's shoulders. "We're going to try. I can't make any promises."

"But what if I ask Santa?"

"These mommy and daddy things are difficult even for Santa. He has an army of elves that help build and deliver toys. I don't know if his helpers can change someone's heart."

"Then I'm going to ask Jesus."

"That's a great idea." She stood and gathered her packages. "How would you two like a hot chocolate?"

Annie sipped her hot tea while she waited in the Bon Air Café for what she hoped would be a whirlwind of activity. The silence before the storm. Nel had ordered a banana split and was sitting at the lunch counter watching Corrie scoop ice cream and add toppings.

165

Annie checked the time on her cell and called to her, "Nel, almost time."

"Okay."

"Follow me." Corrie lifted the giant sundae and Nel walked behind her to the employee break room. "I'll let you know when the coast is clear."

"Got it." Nel picked up her spoon and dug in.

Corrie winked at Annie and got back to work wiping down the counter. In no time at all Greet came barreling in the café. With a slight look of panic on her face, she rushed to the counter.

"Corrie, have you seen Nel?" Corrie gave her a glazed look. Seeing Annie, she ran to her table. "Annie, I can't find Nel." She held out a piece of paper. "She left me this note."

Annie took it and read, *"Mom, I'm running away from home. Don't worry too much, I'll be safe having ice cream at the diner."*

The door crashed open when Puck flew in. "Corrie! Have you seen Nel?" Corrie shot her eyes toward Annie and Greet and Puck headed there. "Greet, Nel's run away from home. I thought I'd find her here. She left me this note."

Annie took the note and read, *"Dad, I'm running away from home. Don't worry too much, I'll be safe having ice cream at the diner."*

"I got the same note but she's clearly not here," Greet said, filled with worry. "Puck, do you think we drove her to this?"

"No, she's been fine. At least, she's acting fine. Maybe our split has hit her harder than she let on."

"The note said she'd be here," Greet said. "If she's not here, where is she?"

"This is odd," Annie said. "Nel left me a note, too."

"Where is it, what does it say?" Greet and Puck blurted the words together.

Annie pulled a paper from her pocket and read, *"Mom and Dad, Do you remember telling me that dad proposed in the booth by the jukebox? If you want the next clue, go sit there now."*

"What's this all about?" Greet walked to the booth and Puck followed. They sat across from each other. "I'm so worried. What if she's out there alone when the sun goes down? She's only a child."

Puck reached across the table and held her hand. "She's going to be okay, we'll find her. So," he lifted his shoulders, "where's the next clue?"

"I have it here," Annie said and began to read, *"I'm running away from home. Don't worry too much, Grandma knows where I am."*

"Thank God," Puck said, "She's at your mom's house. What does any of this have to do with my proposing to you?"

"I can't think about that right now," Greet said. "Let's go." They flew out the door in search of their daughter.

Nel peeked from the break room and Annie gave her a wink. "Stay here with Corrie. I'm going to follow your parents. Thanks for lending me the bike, Corrie. I'll try and return it in one piece."

Annie watched as Greet and Puck climbed in his vehicle and sped away. She hopped on the borrowed bike knowing she could cut between houses and make it to Maud's before them. When she arrived, Maud was waiting for her in the sitting room.

"They're on the way. Got your note?"

"Right here." Maud waved it in the air. "Hide in the coat closet. You'll be able to see and hear everything."

Annie pulled the closet partway closed just as the front door opened.

"Mom!" Greet and Puck rushed in. "Is Nel here?"

"Calm down you two," Maud said. "No, she isn't here." Puck paced the room and Greet held her palm on her forehead.

"She's left some upsetting notes," Greet said. "We think she's run away from home and we can't find her anywhere."

"Take a breath and have a seat on the sofa," Maud said. "She's left me a note too.

They sat and Maud unfolded the paper. She read, *"Mom and Dad, You told me once your first kiss was while sitting on the couch in Grandma's house."*

"How does she remember those things?" Puck asked. "She's right." He took Greet's hand. "I stole a kiss right here. Your parents were in the kitchen and I was as nervous as a cat in a dog fight."

At hearing those words, Annie quietly put her hand on her heart and knew without a doubt she and Orion were doing the right thing.

"Her note goes on," Maud said. *"I'm running away from home but I'm safe with Miss Valentina."*

"Tina's Gelato Shop," Greet and Puck said in unison. They hopped up and headed for the door.

"Wait a second," Greet said, coming to a stop. "What's going on here? Nel's missing but Puck and I are the only ones even a bit concerned."

"Off to the gelato shop you two." Maud ushered them out the door and Annie emerged from the coat closet.

"Great job, Maud." Annie rushed to the back door. "Here I go again." Hopping on the bike, she road one block south of where Puck was driving and arrived a few minutes ahead of them. "Hi Valentina, they're on the way. Are you ready?"

"Yes, all set." She slid the wrappers off of two paper straws.

"Mind if I hide behind the counter?" Annie asked.

"That's a perfect spot." The shop's owner peered out the window. "Hurry, here they come." With less urgency and growing more suspicious, Greet and Puck walked in.

"Hi Valentina," Greet said. "Any chance Nel's with you? She left us a note and we're having trouble finding her." She looked out the window. "The sun is starting to set and I'm getting worried."

"She's not here but isn't this curious. Your little one left me a note." She found the paper next to the cash register. "I was told only to read it after I've served you both this." She produced a strawberry shake with two straws. "Have a seat here," she motioned to one of the tables and placed the ice cream there. "Shall I read this to you?"

"Yes, please do." Greet said as they sat.

"Mom and Dad," Valentina began, *"Your very first date was here at Tina's Gelato Shop. Mom told me it was one of the most romantic*

evenings she's ever had. Dad could only afford one ice cream and you shared it with two straws."

"Isn't there more?" Puck asked. "She should've left us a clue where to go next to find her."

Annie stifled a giggle while Valentina explained, "I was told not to read the next clue until the strawberry shake is gone." She turned back to the counter. "Enjoy."

Annie sat quietly on the floor behind the coolers. Valentina snuck her a chocolate cone and she licked the creamy treat while eavesdropping on her friends. She heard them reminisce about that first date and recall all the dreams they had. Puck's voice turned sweet and Greet's a bit shy as they spent the quiet time together. Eventually, Annie heard the unmistakable sound of their straws drawing up air as they reached the bottom.

Valentina returned to their table and read, *"I'm running away from home but I'm safe at Menno's house."*

"I should've known he'd be involved somehow," Puck said. "Ready for our next stop?"

"Sounds like we're off to Menno's place," Greet said. "You two were roommates after high school. I'm sure we've told Nel about the times we sat on his front porch or watched football on his television."

"We were at Menno's place when you told me we were going to be parents. Talk about a mix of emotions."

"You went pale and almost passed out." Greet giggled. She took his hands and looked up at the man she loved. "You've been such a great dad. Nel's lucky to have you."

"Us. She's lucky to have us and we're going to work this out. We're going to be a family again."

Annie couldn't see them but she was sure Greet was weeping in Puck's shoulder. He patted her back, comforting her. After she heard the bell over the door ping, she emerged from her hiding spot.

"Valentina, you were perfect. Thanks for helping us out."

"I'm glad to do it. Are you off to Menno's place?"

"No, I'm sure they'll make it there. Menno will give them the last clue. It's going to send them down to the lighthouse where Maud is currently waiting with Nel." She looked outside at the darkening sky. "It's the final stop."

"Very clever of you," she said. "From the looks of them tonight I think your plan is going to work."

"Orion dropped Maud and Nel off at the lighthouse but needed to get back home."

"Yes, we have our book club tonight," Valentina explained. "We call it, *Read Between the Wines*. We're meeting at Orion's shop, so she needs to be there to let us inside."

"I'm going back to the house now to get Greet's car. I'll pick up Nel and Maud. We wanted to let Greet and Puck have a quiet evening alone at the lighthouse. It's the perfect spot to fall back in love."

Chapter Sixteen

The well-executed plan seemed to be working. Annie felt really alive as she drove down the now darkening street toward the Willemstoren lighthouse. They had done it. By now, Greet and Puck had arrived there to find Nel safe and sound with her grandmother. The scavenger hunt was over, leaving a renewed love in its place.

She slowed the car as she neared the lofty beacon, it's light cutting a bright beam into the night sky. There was a fire burning near the water. "So romantic. Good idea Maud." Slumping back in her seat, she cut the engine and let herself relax. The running around was over and the mission had been accomplished.

She watched the lantern room. A flash, "One, two, three," she counted, "eight, nine." Another flash. She grinned. "So constant, forever reliable. It's hard to imagine you've been right here, flashing your warning, for all these years." It blinked again. "One two three," she finished, "eight, nine, flash. How many eyes have peered up at you? How many boats at sea?" She watched the light a few more minutes then began to search the area. Not seeing anyone on the beach, she climbed out and walked toward the towering structure. An unexpected figure emerged from the shadow.

"Daddy?" Her chest tightened and she looked around for her friends. "Is Nel with you?"

"No. She's not here." Tak checked his watch. "She's safe at home where Greet and Puck should be arriving right about now."

"I don't understand."

"Orion changed the ending. Your scavenger hunt ends here, with me." Uncertain, he added, "if you'll stay." He motioned toward the fire where two chairs had been set. "We can talk. I owe you much more than that, but I don't know where else to start."

———

Annie stood by the chair and glanced back at her car, her fingernails digging into her palms. Orion had trapped her in her own game. The sky grew black as she watched her father stoke the fire and add another log. He moved slowly, the years of hard labor on the water catching up to him. She remembered him as a large, strong man, but time had whittled away some of his strength. Or perhaps it was his broken heart that stole his resiliency. The night was silent except for the waves spilling on shore and the crackling fire.

"Please sit, Annie." Tak gestured toward her chair as he sat. Neither one spoke and after an awkward amount of silence, he began. "We spent a lot of time here as a family. Your mother said it was the only beach left not discovered by visitors. It's so far south, they don't bother driving down here." He ran his hand threw his scraggly hair and over his heavy beard. "I haven't been here in ages. Maybe since before you left."

"I didn't leave, Daddy," Annie said. "I was sent away, by you. Forgive me if I don't join you on your trip down memory lane. Thinking of my childhood and my life here only brings me sadness. I've worked hard to try and forget it all."

"I'm—" He cleared his throat and shifted in his chair. "I'm sorry to hear that."

More uncomfortable quietness. When it became clear to her that he wasn't going to acknowledge the truth, Annie stood and looked toward the car.

"This was a rotten trick set up by Orion. I don't need to play along."

"You're right," he blurted. "I made you leave. Stay, please. You don't owe me anything, but I'll ask for your patience. I'm trying. It's hard for me to find the words I want to say."

"Maybe you could start by explaining how you could let your only daughter be taken away. I loved you so much. You always said we were best mates." She yelled, "You gave me away!" He nodded and she sat, shaking. "Mom would never have done something like that." She whispered, "She would've done everything she could to keep me."

"Your mom loved you so much. I only pray she understands what I did was for your best interest. No, you're right, she wouldn't have done the same."

"You gave me to Aunt Peggy and Uncle Joe without a second thought." Heat crept up her neck and burned her head. "They never wanted kids and they were stuck with me. Do you know how hard that was to live with?"

"I'm so sorry." His knee jumped repeatedly. "When Rose died, I lost my head. It was as though I was no longer in control of my own thoughts. A dark storm cloud settled over me and hung with me even on sun filled days. I told myself to wake up, move on, keep going, but —" He ran his hand over his face. "I couldn't shake the gloom. There was no joy in life. I sank into my sadness, welcomed it even." He swiped at his tears. "I didn't know if I could go on living."

"Oh, daddy." She let her anger go as she studied her hands and realized the truth. "I'm sorry too. You had no control over the depression that set in." She'd wanted to blame her father for his weakness, but the reality was, he needed help that never came. "I don't imagine you knew what was happening to you. You didn't know you could seek treatment from a doctor."

"There was no help for me," he said. "I had to let you go. I thought, if Rose couldn't raise you, then her brother Joe could. I was so afraid my darkness would creep and spread to you. I couldn't take that chance." He leaned forward in the chair and found her eyes. "I never meant to hurt my best mate. I only ever wanted you to have a chance at a happy life."

"Aunt Peggy and Uncle Joe provided a loving home. I've managed to fill the empty spaces. But Daddy, so much time has gone by. I don't even know you anymore."

"That's not true. I've worked hard to get myself back together. Father O'Brian helped me to understand that Rose's life on earth may have ended, but I'll see her again one day. It's my job now to live a good life, help others, be charitable. I hope my fresh start will include you. If you agree, I promise to be strong again, for you."

Tears ran freely down her cheeks. Her shoulders shook and she began to sob. The fire went blurry in her eyes. Strong arms were around her and she stood to sink into his embrace. The light flashed and she knew, like the lighthouse, her father would once again be a steady, reliable comfort in her life.

The fire was only smoldering kindle when they folded up their chairs. Both emotionally exhausted, Annie's father took her hand and they lumbered toward their vehicles.

"Thank you for talking with me," he said. "I've dreamed of this night for so many years. One day when my Annie would come back home. I'm worn out, but in a good way."

"I know what you mean." She squeezed his hand. "I feel drained too."

"Would you like to see the house?" he asked. "I haven't touched your room. It's just like the day you left."

"You mean Pharrell Williams' *Happy* poster is still hanging over my bed?" She smiled.

"Let's get together again soon." He dropped the tailgate and put the chairs in the bed.

"Soon?" *Focus, Annie.* "Gosh, Dad, I'd like that, but I'm expected home for Christmas. Aunt Peggy made us a reservation." *I need to get back to work and close this deal.*

"You're not staying?" He shut the hatchback. "I thought you came back to—"

"I'm not staying, I'm visiting. Unfortunately, my flight home this morning took off without me. I just need to book another one. I'm closing a huge merger at the bank after the first of the year. I'll be promoted, given a corner office and a sizable pay increase." When she didn't get any response, she continued, "It's a pretty big deal, Dad. You should be proud of me. I'll be married this spring and—"

"We have banks on the island. You could stay here. What about you and Menno—"

"You don't understand, I'm not a teller, I'm an investment banker at one of the largest companies in its industry. This deal going through will make my career. And there is no me and Menno. I'm engaged to a man named Stewart. He's perfect for me, very successful and on a great career path."

"I am proud of you. You've done so well." He squinted, seeing his daughter clearly for the first time after all these years. "Is making money that important to you?"

"No, Daddy, you don't understand. It isn't about the money at all, not really."

"What then?"

"I can't believe I have to explain this to you. It's about the independence that comes with having money. It gives me control over my life. No one will ever rip me out of it again. You, of all people, should get that."

Chapter Seventeen

"Shh." Nel giggled. "They're still sleeping." She poured cereal into her bowl and found milk in the refrigerator. Annie helped herself to a coffee and joined her niece at the table. "Aunt Annie, Jesus fixed it. I asked him to make my mom and dad in love again and he did."

"Jesus had a little help from you," Annie said. "All those notes you wrote really did the trick."

"Yes, they did." Puck came in the kitchen. "You had us worried to death. Good morning, Annie."

Greet joined them with a shy smile. "We don't know whether to punish you for giving us the scare of our lives or thank you." She searched the cabinets. "Who's ready for pancakes? I'm starving."

"Let me pour you both a cup of coffee." Annie was relieved to see the sparkle returning to her friend's face. She hoped the hearty breakfast would be the first step in putting some weight back on her bones.

"None for me, thanks," Greet said. "I think I'll have orange juice."

"No to coffee?" Annie handed Puck a mug. "That's a first."

"She's supposed to limit her caffeine intake." Puck said, glancing at Annie. "We're going to have a baby."

"I'm going to be a sister?" Nel jumped up, wide eyed, and waited for confirmation.

"Yes, Nel," Greet said. "You get to be a big sister."

Nel ran to her mother and hugged her. Puck put his coffee down and wrapped his arms around them both. Annie watched as the family of three embraced.

"We did it."

"Okay, I'm going broke, but I once again have a flight home." Annie spoke to herself as she touched Accept and Pay. She trotted down the stairs and joined Greet and Corrie who had been waiting for her. Greet and Puck had shared their happy news and Corrie was thrilled for the couple.

Annie checked the airline's app one last time then slid her phone into her pocket. "My flight leaves early tomorrow morning. I'll be back in Manhattan with plenty of time to shower and change for Christmas Eve dinner."

"Have fun," Puck said. "Nel and I are going to spend the rest of the morning in our pajamas." He mussed her hair. "Maybe we'll make some mac and cheese for lunch."

"With cut up hotdogs?" Nel asked.

"I don't know how to make it any other way."

"Sounds like fun." Greet beamed at the site of the two of them. Annie thought she looked a little jealous. Maybe she'd be just as happy staying home with her family. "Corrie and I want some quality girl time with Annie before she starts packing."

They walked a few blocks then took off their shoes before stepping onto the cool sand. It was early and the beach was empty, the sky a powder blue. The sun had yet to reach its height and the three cast long shadows as they strolled.

"So, I'll plan to stay with you in New York this spring," Corrie said. "I've got my resume together. Now I'm gathering company names I may be interested in reaching out to."

"Let me know if you need help with any research," Annie said. "I shot my aunt a text last night and she's super excited to have you stay. She wasn't very happy with me not having a flight home. But I went ahead and booked one this morning."

"I can't wait to get there," Corrie said. "With all the drama Greet and Puck caused, we hardly had any time to just have fun together."

"Sorry about that," Greet said. "It was only my marriage falling apart. Besides, you've had plenty of your own tragedies I've had to deal with."

"What? No way, name one."

"Did you, or did you not call me from the donkey sanctuary in the middle of the night in need of a change of clothes?"

"I've got to hear this," Annie said.

"That was nothing, really," Corrie said. "It could've happened to anyone."

"I'll bite," Annie said. "What, exactly could've happened to anyone?"

"Let me tell it," Greet broke in. She took Annie's hand and walked backward in front of her. "I don't want Corrie to leave out any sordid details. This fall Corrie gets asked on a date by one of her co-workers. Only this guy is strapped for cash and takes her to the donkey sanctuary for their date."

"It was a romantic gesture." Corrie stopped walking and Greet continued.

"Romance, sure. The sun sets and Corrie and this guy find themselves 'making hay' in one of the fields."

"Corrie! You did not!" Annie laughed. "On the first date?"

"Yes, she did." Greet took Corrie's hand. "Only, it wasn't an empty paddock, the donkeys found her dress and showed it who's boss."

"They tore the thing into a million pieces," Corrie added. "Rotten beasts."

"Corrie!" They laughed and turned in a circle, feet sinking in the deep sand.

"I'm not even sure you properly thanked me for saving your naked butt."

"Thank you, Greet. You're a true friend."

As the morning warmed, they walked through the shallows and picked up pretty shells they found along the way. Annie told them about her life in New York and how different it was there. When she mentioned she took the subway every day, Corrie wanted to know if she rode into work with her friends. She then asked about the Statue of Liberty and wondered if Annie could see it from her office on Wall Street. Annie explained the massive number of sky scrapers blocked her view of the Hudson.

"I can't wait to get there," Corrie said. "Then I can see for myself."

Greet asked questions about Stewart and his family and wanted to know details about the wedding. Annie found herself lacking in the finer points and explained her Aunt Peggy was in charge of the planning. She and Stewart only needed to show up at the church. Wasn't that wonderful?

The sun was directly overhead when they headed back toward town. They purposefully avoided the snowy blocks and bought sandwiches from a small deli. They sat on a bench on the main road and enjoyed the goings-on in the wintery street a block away. The snow machines diligently cranked out flakes. The square had now accumulated over two feet.

"Look at all that snow," Corrie said. "The kids are having a blast. Let's eat up and go join them."

"Are you crazy?" Greet said, unwrapping her sub. "We're not dressed for that amount of cold. Besides, I'm starving."

"Are you going to be zero fun this entire pregnancy?" Corrie took a big bite of her Ruben. The sauerkraut hung from her mouth until she managed to capture it with her tongue. Chewing, she held up her index indicating she had more to say. "I don't mean to sound selfish, but we do have a *Never Have I Ever* all-nighter planned with my sister and the girls from *Coastal Travel*. Now that you and Puck are back together, I bet you're going to no-show on us."

"I'll be there," Greet assured her. "I love that game. Besides, I've got seven more months to be pregnant and an entire lifetime with Puck."

Annie was ready to devour the turkey club she held with two hands, but the mention of the game left her mouth dry. "Let's finish lunch then I'll go play in the snow with Corrie."

"You're the best," Corrie said, wiping her chin with the back of her hand.

"Okay, okay," Greet said. "I'll go along too."

Once they had eaten their sandwiches and disposed of the trash, they walked the single block to the center of town. Flakes blew from every rooftop and machines hummed on the sidewalks pelting passersby. Children wearing knit hats and mittens played in the snow with rosy cheeks and youthful enthusiasm. The square was peppered with sculptures and fortresses. Lost scarves hung from the lampposts.

"This park is sorely lacking snow angels," Annie stood with her hands on her hips at the edge of the drifts. "Do these island kids not know the importance of the traditional angel made from snow? This is outrageous."

"I think we all know what needs to be done." Corrie said, taking off at a run. As she hit the snow, she squealed, "Let's do this!" With Annie and Greet behind her, and arms held straight out, they stopped and fell backward into the fluffy bed.

"Work your arms girls!" Annie yelled. "And don't forget the legs. Up, down, up, down, we're doing it!"

They attracted the attention of some school kids who stood over them as they worked the snow. Worn out, the three hopped up out of their creations and proudly showed the youngsters what they had made. Several ran off to give it a try themselves.

The three admired their work and laughed at the one-winged angel Corrie had produced.

"I couldn't get the snow to move," she laughed. "It was too heavy."

"That is one sad angel," Annie teased. Before she knew what hit her, Annie was back in the snow with Corrie on top of her. "Stop," Annie laughed as her friend dropped snow down her shirt. "Too cold! Too cold!" She giggled.

"Is that her?" A familiar voice came from the edge of the snow.

"No, that's not Annie." A woman with a distinct New York accent said.

"I think that is Annie." Stewart's low voice was familiar.

"What's happened to her hair?" Aunt Peggy asked.

"Corrie, stop, please." Annie struggled to upright herself. From her view in the snow, she saw three designer woolen coats and proper winter boots. She followed the jackets upward and was shocked to see her family. "Uncle Joe? Aunt Peggy?" Corrie offered her a hand and pulled her to her feet. "Stewart, what are you all doing here?" Annie swiped at the snow now stuck to every inch of her.

"We've come to bring you home," Aunt Peggy said.

"But I just got here." Annie didn't recognize her own voice. She sounded like a child.

"Annie, tomorrow is Christmas Eve," Uncle Joe said. "We expected you home days ago."

"I missed one of my flights and had to reschedule the others a few times." She gestured at Greet who was clearly having a wonderful time in the snow. "Greet's worse off than I thought. I mean, she was. She's better now." Her voice trailed off. "We fixed it."

"Well, we're glad everything has worked out," Aunt Peggy said. "We have a flight that leaves in a few hours and all four of us need to be on it."

"Wait, what?" Annie's phone buzzed. Her feet were beginning to freeze but she could only stand and stare. Her flight was set for tomorrow, not today. She just got here. Her cell buzzed again but still she didn't notice it. How odd to see these people on Bonaire. It was like a dream.

"Annie," Greet said. "Your phone."

"Oh, thanks." She fished it from her pocket and touched Accept. "Richard, hello. Is everything okay?" She listened as her boss delivered the news she dreamt of hearing. "Really?" She straightened and looked at her uncle. "They did?" She glanced at her aunt who smiled back at her and noticed Stewart was growing impatient. "Thank you for calling Richard. We're on our way back tonight. I'll be in the office on the twenty-sixth, bright and early." Richard responded and Annie replied, "Merry Christmas to you as well."

She slid her phone into her pocket. "I did it. They signed early. I got associate." She looked at the family in front of her. How odd that her feet were so cold while a heat burned in her core and climbed up her neck and head. Perspiration speckled her forehead. A darkness engulfed Stewart and she tried to blink it away. Her uncle swayed, or was that her? Aunt Peggy went fuzzy and Annie's head hit the snow.

Chapter Eighteen

"There you are."

Annie woke to a concerned face looking down at her. She had been changed out of her snow covered clothes and was now nice and warm in her bed. The gooseberry walls had become her sanctuary and she knew she was safe. She pushed herself into a sitting position and found she was wearing a pair of Greet's sweats.

"Aunt Peggy." Memories of the afternoon came washing back. "What happened? How did I get here?"

"You fainted in the snow," her aunt said. "It's no wonder. Running around like a school child wore you out. How are you feeling?"

She took a moment to assess herself. "I feel fine. Well rested, actually."

"We were able to walk you back here. You were pretty out of it but Greet and I got you changed and put you to bed. You've been sleeping for almost an hour. Dr. Stevenson wants us to call her back if you're not feeling well."

Annie sat on the side of the bed and stretched. Uncle Joe tapped on the door.

"May I come in?" he asked.

"Yes Joe, she's up," Aunt Peggy said. "I'm just packing her things."

"How are you feeling? You gave us quite a scare." He sat next to her and put his hand on her back. "We thought it would be a nice surprise for you, seeing us all here, but maybe we should've called first. I think the excitement of seeing your fiancé was a bit too much."

"Stewart." Annie said.

"He's downstairs with a crowd of people who are all waiting to say goodbye."

"Goodbye?"

"Yes, Annie," Aunt Peggy said as she folded clothes and laid them in the roller bag. "We're going home. Joe, why don't you leave us and let me help her get dressed."

"I know when I'm not needed." He stood and patted Annie's shoulder. "Let me know when you're packed. I'll carry your bags down the stairs for you." As Uncle Joe left the room, another person walked in.

"Hello Peggy." Maud held two steaming mugs in her hands. "How nice to see you again."

"You know each other?" Annie asked.

"Yes, of course," Aunt Peggy said. "We met Maud at your mom's funeral."

But the way she said it and the chill in the air gave Annie reason to believe it wasn't a cordial meeting.

"Peggy, would you be so kind as to give me a minute alone with Annie?" Maud asked.

"We're on a tight schedule, I'm afraid—"

"It'll only take a moment." Maud smiled, clearly not leaving. Peggy, looking a bit indignant, left the room.

Maud handed Annie a mug and sat next to her on the side of the bed. "I won't take up too much of your time, but I wanted to tell you something before you leave."

"Now you've got me nervous." She sat with one leg bent and leaned back on the shams. She blew on the tea and took a sip. "What is it?"

Before Rose died, she asked me to promise her something. I'll never forgive myself for not seeing it through."

"What did she ask of you?"

"I think you know. Do you remember after the funeral, Joe, Peggy and I exchanged some harsh words."

"At the time I knew you were upset with them. I'm not sure I understood why."

"When Rose knew in her heart she'd be leaving us, she asked me to help Tak with raising you. She knew you'd need a woman in your life and I always thought of you as my second daughter. I promised her I'd help take care of you." She placed her palm on Annie's knee. "I failed her."

"No Maud, not you. It was my father's responsibility."

"I'm afraid by then your father had sunken too low. We all knew you needed someone to take you in. I'd promised your mom I'd look out for you and planned to do just that."

"You wanted custody of me?"

"Yes, but your Uncle Joe wouldn't have it. He insisted on taking you. Being a blood relation, he held all the cards."

"Really? He fought to have custody of me?" She slumped back. "I had no idea. I always felt like such a burden to them."

"Oh, on the contrary. He thought getting you off Bonaire and to a more metropolitan location would benefit you. I remember when he started spouting off colleges and universities that would be on your horizon. Insisting that the culture available every day in Manhattan would inspire you to flourish among it."

Annie felt her heart lift. All those years she felt like a stone in their shoe. Working so hard to quietly slip through each day. Pushing herself to become a top student and joining clubs and teams she thought would please them.

"He was right," Annie said. "The city offered me all of those things. Opportunities I never would've had."

"Your aunt and uncle have raised a wonderful and caring young woman with a heart as big as the island. They've done well by you."

———

Annie sat on the chair in front of the vanity as Aunt Peggy stood behind her and fixed her hair. She tugged at the suit jacket that seemed to be cutting off her circulation. She slipped her feet in and out of the heels that now pinched her toes. Strands of her hair pulled at her scalp and she couldn't help but reach up and itch it.

"You've let this hair go wild. I can hardly capture it all in the bun."

"All packed?" Uncle Joe came in. "I can take this downstairs." He looked at his niece. "Well, look at you. The new associate is ready for the streets of Manhattan again."

Annie studied herself in the mirror. If it weren't for her tanned face, no one would know she'd been on Bonaire. Her shirt was starched and the pantsuit dark against it. Aunt Peggy added the elastic and claimed her hair tamed. She forced a smile but her eyes told a different story.

"Annie," Uncle Joe said. "Are you okay?"

"Of course she is," Aunt Peggy said. "Just look at her. She's perfect."

"Peggy, do you mind?"

"Is something wrong?" Peggy checked the time. "We should leave for the airport soon. Buck has offered to give us a ride."

"Puck," Annie said. "His name is Puck. He and Greet are expecting."

Joe looked at Peggy and nodded toward the door.

"I'll let you two talk," she said while leaving the room. "I'm sure you need to catch up on what's happening on Wall Street."

Joe sat on the bed and Annie turned toward him. He took her hands in his. "My parents had the hardest time raising your mother." He smiled. "I was the older brother who got straight A's and followed all the rules. Rose, not so much. Your mom was a free spirit. My father tried to push her into finance, but she'd have none of it. I spent my summers, like you, interning at World Global Bank while she was picketing the sale of whale meat overseas. She had a true love of nature and the ocean.

"Mom told me about her volunteer work with Greenpeace." Annie smiled, remembering. "It all sounded so romantic somehow."

"She may not have lived a long life, but it was a full one." He squeezed her hands and seemed to have trouble saying the next few words. They came out one at a time. "I don't know if you're living the life she meant for you to have. I think maybe she'd be upset with me for—"

"Uncle Joe, you've given me everything. Look at me." She grinned and straightened. "Associate with the corner office at age twenty-seven. It's a dream come true."

"But are you sure it's your dream and not one you borrowed from me?"

"I..." Annie turned and looked at her reflection. "I've always wanted to make you proud. You and Aunt Peggy." She saw the sorrow on her uncle's face behind her. "But I think I've found what I love to do. High finance is exhilarating."

"Annie, I just—"

"Now let's go say our farewells." She stood. "I'd hate to miss another plane."

––––––––

Annie held her head high as she descended the stairs. She would make her goodbye to Menno short and sweet. It had been wonderful seeing her old friend again. She'd do better at keeping in touch, but it was time to go. Her plan was basically the same with her dad. A quick 'so long' and out the door.

Her heels clicked on each step. She stopped at the bottom and surveyed the room. Neither Menno nor her father was there. Even as her heart was sinking, she raised her head and smiled.

"Annie." Orion approached her with her arms out. Annie sunk into them and closing her eyes, breathed in the scent that reminded her of her mother.

"Thank you for everything." Annie looked at Rose's friend. She fought the tears she felt building. "I made associate, I've got to get back home."

"Your mother would be so proud." Orion dabbed at her eyes and stepped away.

"Maud." Annie hugged the woman she knew she'd miss the most. "I want to—" But she began to sob in the crook of her neck. Maud held her until she got her tears under control.

"Don't wait another ten years Annie," Maud said. "You'll have a new niece or nephew soon and they'll want to know their Aunt Annie."

Annie could only manage a nod. Her throat had grown tight and her vision was blurred. She turned away only to be crashed into by Nel.

"Don't go Aunt Annie." She buried her red face in her aunt's side. "You told us you don't have any friends. But you do. We're your friends." She looked up full of hope. "Please stay."

"Nel, I—" Tears ran into her mouth and her nose filled. "It's time for me to go."

Nel ran to her father who held her as she cried.

Stewart stood by the front door and when Annie caught his eye, he tapped on his wrist. She nodded then found Greet. The two held each other as though the world itself was trying to pull them apart.

"I love you, Greet," Annie whispered in her ear.

"I love you too." Greet pulled back and looked at her friend, her sister. "It feels good to say it, doesn't it? Annie, if you love someone, be sure to tell them."

Annie sat next to Stewart in the first class section of the plane waiting to take off. Aunt Peggy and Uncle Joe sat directly behind them. Stewart placed his laptop on the tray table and worked on something Annie assumed was election related. Twice, he told her he was glad to finally have her coming home.

The flight attendant stopped in the aisle and asked him to stow the computer for take-off.

"What's the sense in having these first class tickets if I still need to follow the rules of the unwashed masses?" He slammed the unit closed. "I may as well be seated in coach."

Annie patted his knee and looked out her window. The flamingo pink terminal laughed at her and the clear sapphire sky smiled. She was wrapped in her heavy winter coat heading north. Of course she was the butt of their joke. Her cell buzzed causing her to jump. She'd yet to turn it off or put in in airplane mode. She checked the screen. *Unknown caller* with a Bonaire number. Menno must've found out she was gone. She touched Decline, powered it down, and put it away.

Chapter Nineteen

"**A**bsolutely not!" Orion was mortified at what her friend Dimphy had in mind. "You can't register to be in the pageant, it's for the kids."

"They have a senior division, it's right there on the entry form." Dimphy wiggled into a red satin bustier with white feathers along the fitted bodice. She sat on her bed and pulled on black thigh-high leather boots then zipped them up the back. "You could join with me but that muumuu isn't going to win you any points."

Orion held a paper and studied the contest rules. "The senior division is for high schoolers. Seniors in high school, not seventy-year-olds. I won't let you do this." She pulled the Santa hat off her friend's head.

"Give me that! I'm going to win this contest, with you or without you. I'll be crowned *Little Miss Snowflake* if you like it or not." She snatched her hat back and tromped out of the room.

Chapter Twenty

The sun was setting on Christmas Eve. Families gathered at the elementary school waiting to enter the festival of lights that would take them to the town center. A brilliantly lit archway beckoned to them as they awaited Santa's instructions.

"Excuse me, pardon me." Annie pushed her way through the crowd searching for the man she loved. She was desperate to find him. "I'm sorry, excuse me please." She bumped elbows and may have stepped on a toe or two as she navigated toward the arch. The crowd thinned and she saw him. Menno, wearing a complete Santa Claus outfit stood with her father and Maud. They were chatting and waiting for the moment he would lead the families thru the pathway of lights. They saw her as she burst free from the crowd. Their jaws dropped and eyes grew wide. She stopped, gathered her thoughts, and approached them.

"I'm sorry. I owe you an apology." She caught her breath. "It all happened so fast. The plane's doors were about to close when I knew I had to get off. I..." she huffed. "I broke it off with Stewart, I want to be here, with you."

He stared at her and pure wonder seemed to wash over him.

Annie saw the moment he realized what she was saying and he seemed to be overcome. His shoulders fell and his face shone with a peaceful ease of mind. Finally, what he'd waited all these years for. His Annie was coming home.

"I love you. I've always loved you," Annie continued. "I never stopped. Dreams of living my life with you filled my nights and coming home to Bonaire filled my thoughts during the day." She inhaled and considered her next words. "The first time I left you, I had no choice. My heart was shattered. Why would I ever choose to leave you again?" She bolted forward and wrapped her arms around her father. "I love you, Daddy."

Father O'Brian called the crowd to order and a hush settled over them. The choir, dressed in their robes, began to sing *Oh Holy Night*. Greet, asked to sing the solo, led them. Her voice started quietly, as if a true angel were among them. Puck took her hand and the other members joined in. The song grew as they began to move forward. Annie held her father's hand and they followed Father O'Brian toward the lighted archway.

Looks of wonder grew on the children's faces as they entered the bright tunnel. They pointed at glowing angels and an illuminated manger scene. As they strolled they sang the solemn hymn. As the procession neared town, snow fell over the line of people and the choir broke into a cheerful *Let It Snow*. There was some commotion behind her and suddenly Annie was wrapped in a four person hug. Greet, Corrie and Nel had found her and with teary faces, each proclaimed that they knew she would be back.

Nel smiled up at her. "You came home."

"Yes, Nel, I'm home."

Menno turned and winked at Annie. He raised his arms and shouted, "Merry Christmas!" The multitude reached the end of the lights and walked into the square. The children ran off into the snow while their parents manned tables of hot chocolate and gingerbread cookies.

The enormous tree stood like a beacon in the center of the park. Many children naturally ran toward it. Glimmering with lights, and in true island fashion, a starfish shone from the top. Colorfully wrapped presents were tucked underneath the lowest branches. Near the base of the evergreen sat Santa's red quilted chair. It waited for the jolly old man to take his throne. Some eager young ones were already gathered around it.

"I'm on duty until I've handed out all those gifts," Menno said. "I could use a hand if you're available."

"Go ahead Annie," Tak said. "I'm volunteering with Puck at the food donation pick up." He nodded toward the edge of the park where Puck was loading care packages into the vehicles of families in need.

"Okay then," Annie said. "I'll see you later Daddy." She watched him go and wasn't sure if she was imagining a new pep in his step. She then smiled up at the white bearded man. "It looks like I'm all yours."

Santa took his chair to cheers from his young fans. They all gathered around while Menno read the beloved story, *The Night Before Christmas*. The kids heard the story every year but never seemed to grow tired of it. As he finished the book, Annie handed him a package from under the tree.

"Let's hope you're all on my nice list this year." He read the tag, "Charlie, this one's for you."

Snowball Charlie jumped up and sprang toward Santa. He thanked him and quickly shredded the gift wrap. "The hover ball! It's just what I wanted."

Annie gave Menno the side eye. How did he know Charlie had asked for that exact gift? She found the next one and as Menno made another child happy, she collected the now destroyed paper and put it in a bag. There was a pattern starting and she was happy to be part of it.

"Nel, this one has your name on it."

"But Santa, you already gave me my gift," Nel said, as she moved forward. "You brought my mom and dad back together. Plus, we're having a baby." She looked closely at the old elf and lowered her brow, "Do you have a twin named Menno?" She tore the paper from the box. "The Disco Dance Mat! Thank you, Santa!"

When all the packages had been cleared from under the tree, Santa wished the children a Merry Christmas and handed each a candy cane. As they dispersed among the crowd, he excused himself and went into the general store to magically change into Menno again. Annie waited for him near the tree.

"There you are." Maud approached with a huge smile. "Merry Christmas."

"It really is, isn't it?" She beamed as snow drifted down around them.

"I've already thanked Orion and I wanted to thank you too." Maud nodded toward Puck, Greet and Nel, all huddled together on a bench enjoying mugs of hot chocolate. "You two were so clever. Coming up with the scavenger hunt was a brilliant idea."

"Maybe the situation just needed a fresh eye," Annie said. "They've always loved each other. Orion and I gave them a little nudge to remind them of that."

"I've offered for them to move in with me," Maud said. "Help to take some of the financial burden off so they can each pursue a degree at the college."

"Maud, that's so nice of you."

"I'm glad you think so but I must admit, it's a little bit of a selfish move." She grinned. "I'm so excited to have a little one on the way. I was thinking of making the office a nursery. Or I could use the back room and move the television out front. What do you think?"

"I think Greets carrying the luckiest baby on the planet. She and Puck for parents." Annie placed her palm on Maud's shoulder. "And you for a grandmother."

"Here comes Menno." She patted Annie's hand. "I don't want to take all of your time." She turned to leave. "Oh, and Annie, welcome home."

"Hey there." Menno returned. "I may not be as popular with the kids, but I'm a lot more comfortable."

"You're still popular in my book," she said, taking his hand and looking up at him. "I'm a little disappointed, though."

"Disappointed? Why?"

"I thought I might kiss a man with a beard tonight." She grinned up at him.

"I can go get it." He threw his thumb at the shop. "I'll be right—"

"Don't you dare." Annie closed her eyes, raised onto her tiptoes, and tilted her chin. She thought the kiss would be familiar, just like old times. But they were different people now, somehow newly in love, and the kiss was filled with passion. She became lost in his arms. Aware of the buzzing crowd, she fell back on her heels.

"Oh, Annie." Menno pushed a lock of hair out of her eyes. "You are my forever, always were, always will be." He wrapped his arms around her and kissed the top of her head. "My prayer has been answered. You've come home to me."

"Care to escort me through the North Pole?" Annie asked.

They strolled lazily among the throngs of people. Children ran in the snow knowing the machines would be turned off soon. Nel and Charlie played with his new toy, their friends all circled around waiting for a turn.

They came upon a crowd cheering quite loudly and walked toward it. "What's going on here?" Annie asked.

"Let's find out."

They worked their way through the throng and to a temporary stage that had been built in the square. A cute toddler was spinning in circles, her tulle dress floating out around her. Next to her stood Dimphy.

Annie wasn't sure if the over exaggerated eye roll Dimphy gave the sweet girl was meant to be seen or not, but she did know that Dimphy's outfit had attracted a crowd. Red bustier and matching mini, and a pair of thigh high black boots with zippers up the back. Her rendition of Mrs. Claus had several white feathers along her hemline. The mother of the tiny ballerina hurried her off stage and the master of ceremonies introduced the next contestant. He asked her the standard question.

Dimphy grabbed his microphone. "What does Christmas mean to me?" She repeated the query then cleared her throat. "Christmas means gifts under the tree, lots of pie and treats, and snow." She smiled at the polite applause and gave the man his mic back. Then she grabbed his hand and added, "And baby Jesus."

"Thank you, Dimphy," the man said. "And what will you be performing as your talent?"

"I'm going to do a dance." And with that, *Santa Baby* began to play.

The men began whistling and cheering her on. Perhaps they had already been enjoying their Christmas cheer. Their wives shot them ugly looks and rammed elbows into their sides.

"Leave it to Dimphy," Annie said. "I love her free spirit but I'm not sure I'm ready for that dance." She squeezed Menno's hand and the two worked their way back out of the enthusiastic audience.

"The church has a live nativity in front of the bell tower. Would you like to see it?"

"Yes, that sounds great."

They laughed as they stood in front of the manger scene. Dogs filled in for camels and two goats played the role of the oxen. The donkeys, they got right. Ginger slept on her back in the hay, four paws heavenward. The little boy playing Joseph dropped his staff and went to lay next to her.

"How are you two doing? Enjoying the nativity?" Tak joined them in front of the church just as Father O'Brian called the crowd to come near.

"Hi Daddy. You're just on time. Father O'Brian is getting ready to start."

It was dark and the sky was full of stars and snowflakes. The choir gathered in front of the church and Greet, with a renewed joy, stood among them. When they sang out the first few lines of *Silent Night*, more people gathered around. They were all invited to join in and sing with the choir. Annie sang with happy tears in her eyes.

Her life had come full circle. She was fortunate to have grown up surrounded by family and friends on the beautiful island of Bonaire. When the world threw her a curve ball, she regrouped and started again. With the loving support of her aunt and uncle, she lived a successful and fulfilled life. But perhaps someone above suspected her world was out of kilter. Unforeseen events ultimately put her back where she belonged. Back where her mother knew she should be, back beside her father. Or perhaps, it was all simply the magic of Christmas.

As the beloved hymn came to an end, the church bells rang out. Father O'Brian raised his arms and welcomed everyone to the celebration of the birth of their Savior. He opened the church doors and received his congregation. Annie held Menno's hand and placed her other on her father's back. Together, the three walked into San Bernardo Church.

About the Author

I hope you enjoyed spending Christmas in Bonaire. I'm currently in North Carolina writing my fifth novel, a wholesome tale of a woman whose life just took a turn. Developing characters readers want to cheer for is my goal.

When I'm not writing, I work as a dental hygienist, a job I've loved for over thirty years! During my free time, you'll find me below the ocean's surface, diving the reefs surrounding my beloved Bonaire Island. Maybe I'll see you there sometime!

Please join my mailing list at the link below. You'll receive a free short story and get behind the scene information. Questions about characters or plot? Get them answered here. Interested in joining my ARC and launch teams? Here is where you'll gain entry into those groups.

Thank you for reading,

Anne

https://dashboard.mailerlite.com/forms/943918/ 124862357273838711/share

Made in the USA
Las Vegas, NV
22 September 2024

95637283R00115